BLACK REIGN PUBLISHING

PAIN & PLEASURE

A story of Sex, Money, & Misery

By. Ty ROBINSON

AF372178

Copyright © 2021 Black Reign Publishing

All rights reserved. Without limiting the rights under copyright reserved. No part of this book may be reproduced, stored in any or introduced into a retrieval system, to transmitted in any form, or by any means (Electronic, mechanical, photocopying, recording, or otherwise), without prior written consent from both the author and the publisher, except for the brief quotes that are used in literary reviews.

This is a work of fiction. It is not meant to depict, portray or represent any particular real persons. All the characters, incidents and dialogues are the product of the author's imagination and are not to be construed as real. Any references or similarities to actual events, entities, real people (living or dead) or to real locales and/or to any particular places of locations are only intended to give this story a sense of realism. Any similarity in names, characters, entities, and incidents are coincidental.

"She called out for love,
to a world of deaf ears.
She reached out a hand for help,
to only grab only air.
Tears on her cheeks,
but no one could see her cry.
A bird with broken wings,
no longer knew how to fly,
She walked out into the world,
with a heart made of ice,
Just another little black girl.
That no longer cared about life."

PROLOGUE

I was both hot and cold as I stared at him. Though I was numb, I felt it all. His hands groping me. The sound of my breathing and heartbeat as my body responded to his touch. My glassy and heavy eyes stared into his as he removed my bra. A cop car sped by outside, but it sounded far off and the distant siren echoed in my brain as it faded away. Inside of this motel room, I sat edge of the bed, staring at this kind of cute, horny ass motherfucker that picked me up at a bar on Sunset Boulevard. It didn't take much for him to get me to leave with him. A few drinks, some bullshit conversation, and after I did a bump of coke in the ladies' room; I left with him. Now, he had me naked from the waist up, sucking on my left titty while squeezing the right one. Pinching my pierced nipple. I put my hands behind me on the bed, leaned back, and stared up at the ceiling. Feeling nothing. Russell, whatever the Hell his last name is, was enjoying himself. I wasn't. He was the one turned on. Satisfying his lust. I was just here.

Neither happy or sad. Angry or revulsed. This lame ass, half black-half white, ring wearing married man feasted on my breasts. He sucked and licked on my tits hard and rough. Covering them in saliva. Russell was so into engorging himself on my titties that he was oblivious to my sigh. Of boredom. Of indifference. Part of me wanted to push him off of me, grab my shirt-jacket-and bra, then run out of the door. I didn't though. I just sat there as this motherfucker went from one tit to the other until he was pleased. With my breasts covered in spit, he pushed me onto my back and began to undo my jeans. I offered up zero resistance as he pulled my jeans off to discover that I wasn't wearing underwear. As he pushed my legs open, I stared at the wall on the left side of the room. Knowing knew what this thirsty motherfucker was staring at. My smoothly shaved pussy. I didn't react when his anxious fingers began probing it. I kept staring at the wall as his breathing increased. He toyed with my clit and pussy lips. Even when I felt his fingers sliding inside me, I still didn't move. I just lied there.

It was Russell's lucky night. He maneuvered me on the bed to eat me out and that's what he did. For a long ass time. He held my legs up by the back of my thighs with his face buried in my pussy. Sucking, licking, and slurping. He also moaned while babbling. In between eating it, he told me how sweet my pussy tasted. How wet it was. How warm it was. I never responded though. I had closed my eyes and despite him putting my hands on his head as he ate me; I didn't encourage him. I didn't moan, rock my hips, or pull his face in deeper. I didn't enjoy what he was doing to me, but I didn't stop him either. This, what was happening, was the only thing men wanted from me. Sex. Pussy. The pleasure of tasting, savoring, and enjoying it. This IS what I am was in this world. An instrument of someone else's enjoyment. I opened my eyes a little when Russell was finished gorging himself on me. He quickly rolled a condom on, crawled on top of me, pushed my legs open, and I lied there staring at the wall through half open eyes. As his five, six-inch penis penetrated me.

After about a minute of Russell rabbit humping away on top of me, I turned my head forward to look at him. My arms were back, hands by my head as he banged away inside me while staring down at my face. Sweat forming all over his, expression twisted in fiery lust, and he was moaning. Loud. When he came down to kiss me, it was one sided. My lips parted as I let him slide his tongue into my mouth. He sucked on my bottom lip, bit it a little, and then he went all in me. I didn't moan like I used to when he grabbed my hair and twisted my head and neck. I didn't react when he locked his hand around my throat. Squeezing hard enough to slow the flow of my air, but not hard enough to actually hurt or strangle me. Russell was loud as fuck as he stroked away inside me. Fucking me was paradise for him. He was in Heaven.

Despite not being turned on and his just below average dick did nothing for me; I couldn't fight the nature of my body. I always get extremely wet during sex. My pussy was sopping and each stroke of his penis ended with a slurpy squish. I could see that the feeling and sound of all that juiciness between my legs was driving Russell out of his mind. He was stroking hard, fast, and with one hand fisting my hair. Torqueing my head back and to the right; his other hand locked on my titty. He hammered his dick into me until he screamed that he was cumming. I turned my head to the side and closed my eyes. Lying there like a fallen statue as he busted off inside the condom.

He lied on top of me for a while before getting his ass up and making his way for the bathroom. By the time he returned from taking a piss, then a quick shower; I was sitting next to the window. I only had my shirt on as I smoked a cigarette. For some reason, he explained to me that under different circumstances, he would spend the night with me; but he had to go. It was late and he had to be up for work at seven am. I understood, right? He was waiting for an answer that wasn't coming. I kept staring at the parking lot of the motel as I exhaled smoke towards the window. Instead of answering him, without looking at his pathetic ass, I simply told him to leave my money on the dresser and go home to his wife. Now that he's washed the aroma of my pussy off of him. I kept sitting there at there at the window even after the door opened, he exited, and the door shut. It was quiet again, but the silence was just as loud as the noise to me.

I sat there with my hand on my head, looking out the window, not really focused on anything. Trying to feel nothing. That was impossible. I tried to ignore, deny, and not acknowledge everything that I felt; but there they were. Toxic thoughts and feelings stacked up in my psyche. As slow tears began to trickle down my cheeks, I didn't even bother wiping them away. I allowed them to fall as I lit another Newport. As much as I wanted to resist what I felt, I was too tired to fight my emotions. My tears flowed harder as the depression that was always there stabbed my soul.

The anger that's been with me since I was child flamed in my heart. The sadness that often strangled me was slowly wrapping its hands around my throat. I began to sob as I took a hard drag on my cigarette, feeling it all. Shame, worthlessness, dirty, hollow, and lonely. I had no family that loved me, true friends that I could rely on, or any meaning in this world. Russell, that thirsty motherfucker I met at the bar was just another man in a long line of them that got what he wanted from me. A nut. That's all I was to them. Just another bitch for them to get their nut off with.

Not long after I stubbed my cigarette out, I stood in front of the mirror in the bathroom. Staring at myself. At my tired and empty, natural honey brown eyes. Without the colored contacts, I could see my soul. It was dark, dull, & full of smoke. The smoke of misery. Tears continued to flow down my cheeks as I stared at a pretty face with an ugly reflection. I wanted to drink this pain away. Smoke and snort this agony away until I was numb. Until I couldn't feel anything anymore. I've tried that, but it didn't last. Those horrible feelings always came back. The thoughts, memories, and pain always came back. I couldn't hold it in any longer. I buried my face in my hands and cried. Hard. I just wanted all of it to stop!

Memories of everything I been through for a far as I could remember began flashing through my mind. Sadness and anger fought for dominance in my spirit until anger overpowered the hurt. I moved my hands away from my face, stared at my own reflection for a moment, saw nothing of worth, and decided to erase my own image. I punched the mirror until it shattered. My hands were cut and bleeding, but I didn't care. I screamed as I ripped the shower curtain down, punched and kicked the wall several times, then collapsed onto my knees. Holding myself as I bawled. My own mind was like a torturer that I could never escape. I was haunted, scarred, broken, and trapped. Trapped in life, when death would be my salvation.

I was hyperventilating as I looked down at a long shard of glass on the floor. I grabbed it, sat back, and held up my left arm. I stared at the skin of my wrist, gripped the blade of mirror, and wanted to end it all. My death would be a controversy, but not many would lose sleep that I took my own life. I would be simply another juicy story for the papers and shit. Twenty-five-year-old ex-porn star commits suicide in a Hollywood motel. The twisted fans that jerked off to my videos wouldn't give a shit, the bitches that I worked with in the industry wouldn't care, neither would ninety-nine percent of the general public. I'd be written off as another young black porn actress that killed herself. I pressed the glass into my wrist, embracing the desire to die. Maybe then I'd be at peace. Maybe then I'd be free. Maybe then, I'd be happy. I didn't want to be here. I didn't wanna feel like this anymore. I was miles past tired. I had nothing left to live for. Yet, as I pressed the glass into my skin, ready to end it all….

….my twenty-five-years of life began playing out in my mind like a movie

PART ONE

BROKEN HEART

CHAPTER ONE

"Sweet child raised in a sour world."

Though I've be a resident of Los Angeles, California since I was twenty, for the first half of my life; I was a native of Ohio. Cincinnati to be precise. Long before I was known by my porn moniker, I was simply Shanice. Shanice Landon. My earliest memories began for me around four years old. I remembered my mother, father, my brother, aunts, uncles, grandparents, and cousins. I also recalled the house that I grew up in. It was huge with a lot of dark wood, a spacious back yard, and I specifically remembered the front door. It was crimson red. Once upon a time in my life, I was a happy. My family was close. We always did things together. Cookouts, family reunions, birthday-house parties, and every fall; it was football on Saturday and Sunday's. Most of my family were die-hard fans of Ohio's gridiron teams. The Bengals, Browns, and Ohio State Buckeyes. Between August and February, football was a Landon family tradition. Every weekend, we had on our jersey's. Getting down on chicken wings, snacks, beer, and yelling at the TV in the living room of whoever home we took over for gameday.

My world was beautiful and bright for eight solid years. My mother and father, Cassandra and Nelson Landon, were my joy. My mom was a co-director of a daycare center. I was with her for four straight years until I started school. Daddy worked four jobs throughout the year. In the warm seasons he was a landscaper and he did a little construction work on the side, but during the cold winter months, he worked for the state. He drove a plow truck for the highway road service when it snowed and he pulled down shifts at UPS during the holiday rush. No matter what, my dad worked long and hard all year long to take care of his family. My only sibling, my brother Avery; he was my hero. Though he was four years older than me, he wasn't the typical older brother to a younger sister. He didn't pick on me, tease me, or bully me. We were very close and he did exactly what our father told him to do after I was born. Avery was my protector and he took care of me. When I was old enough to go outside without my parent's supervision, it was my brother that watched over me.

Avery took me to the playground, the corner store, and to my all-time favorite place when I was six years old. Mr. Eddie's pizza shop. Daddy always gave my brother twenty bucks to buy me for pizza, curly fries, and soda. Also, to play the arcade games. I would stand on a chair next to my brother as we had so much fun playing the classics. Mr. Eddie had three of the legendary arcade machines. Pac-Man, Mortal Kombat, and Street Fighter. Avery and I played each one every time we went to get pizza. No matter where my brother and I went, he was my guardian. Always holding my hand, he would carry me on his back, and I always felt safe with my big bro.

At home, even if his friends and our male cousins were hanging out with him; Avery didn't make me go away because I was a girl. I was right there in his bedroom with him and his homies. Playing video games, wrestling, joking around, and having fun. My brother was a football fan like the rest of the family. Though he played wide receiver on a pop-warner team, his true passion was basketball. I went with my brother as much as possible to the courts at the park to watch him play ball. I was eight and Avery was twelve. Watching my bro ball on Saturday afternoons was the highlight of my week. To me and many others, he was a natural born legend in the making. A young phenom on the rise.

He was amazing on the blacktop. Even though he was only twelve years old. My brother had a ball in his hands from the time he could walk. His entire bedroom was decorated in Basketball memorabilia. Posters, large framed portraits of his favorite players, and the Cleveland Cavaliers. His team. At the park, I sat on the bleachers and watched my brother do his thing. Avery could dribble like a master, pass the ball like a magician, his crossover was nasty, and he was able to shoot the lights out. He idolized three players. Michael Jordan, Allen Iverson, and Kobe Bryant. Every single time we went to the park, I was my brother's personal cheerleader. Cheering for him when he scored or did something awesome. When he was done playing with his friends, he played with me. I mostly ran around the court with the ball. Slapping it as he laughed while trying to show me how to dribble it right. I didn't care about learning how to play ball. I was happy to be hanging out with my big brother. Once we were done and it was time to go home, I carried Avery's ball as he held my hand.

Until I was eight years old, my life was good. I had two parents that loved each other and their kids, Avery was my everything, we were being raised in a good home, and my world was perfect. Safe. Filled with love. About six months after my eighth birthday, I was at my best friend

Jamia's house for an all-girls sleepover. It was me, Jamia, and four of our friends. My besties' mom was with us and we had crazy fun. Dressed in pajamas and camping out in the living room. We enjoyed pizza, soda, and popcorn while watching a Hey-Arnold marathon on Nickelodeon. I remember the exact date of that night. June 17th, 2002. It was a Saturday. I had long braids with red & white beads. I went to bed that night full of junk food with Snoopy pajamas on. Jamia and I slept face to face on the floor in her moms' living room. I remember everything from the night of June 17th, because on the 18th, the first act of cruelty from the savage hands of life stole my joy and a large part of my heart.

I was having so much fun at my besties house that I didn't even notice that it was well past noon and my dad hadn't come to pick me up yet. The other girls' folks picked them up, so it was just me and Jamia. We were in her room playing dress up, watching cartoons, and attempting to style each other's hair. For some reason, Jamia's mom kept checking on us. Asking us was everything ok? She specifically kept asking me was I ok? I told her yes each time she asked. Miss Sonja joined us during our eight-year-old hair salon session. After showing us a few things, she took out my beads and re-braided my hair in a cute style. Doing my hair took a long time. I was so preoccupied with sitting in front of Miss Sonja while she did my hair and laughing with Jamia; that I was unaware of the time. It was almost five in the evening. At the dinner table, I asked when was my dad coming to get me? I was supposed to be hanging out with my brother at home. It was Sunday night and my mom let me stay up later than normal to watch the Simpsons with Daddy and Avery. We all loved the Simpsons.

I ended up watching it with Jamia and her parents. I kept asking when was I going home until my mom finally showed up. It was close to ten at night when she knocked on Miss Sonja's door. I was ready to go, but the expression on my moms' face confused me. She had this strange look of sadness, her eyes were red, and her cheeks were tear streaked. As I asked her were we going home, Miss Sonja was leading Jamia across the living room. I watched them walk up the stairs, then I looked at my mother. By my shoulder, she led me to the couch and softly asked me to sit with her. I did, she took my hands, new tears began rolling down her cheeks, and she stared into my eyes for a long time before she shattered my world. My brother was gone. He was dead. Like me, he was staying over at a friends' house. Avery and his best friend Braylon were at the park running full-court with a bunch of boys when they were caught in a crossfire. Two drug dealers shot it out at the park. One saw the other, guns came out, and they opened fire. With a bunch of kids trapped between all those bullets.

Three young black boys were shot. Two were killed. Avery made it all the way to the hospital, but died as the operating room was being set up to save his life. That's why my parents didn't pick me up. Why Miss Sonja was acting weird all day. She knew. Upon hearing that brother was dead, as my mother wrapped her arms around me; I started crying. I didn't stop for a long time. All day and every night until Avery's funeral; I cried. As did my mother and father. My dad was gone too. Though he shed tears for my brother, I saw more anger than sadness in him.

On the day we said goodbye to and buried Avery, daddy rarely spoke. To anyone. It was tears, silence, and a look of darkness in his eyes. My mom held me throughout the entire funeral. I don't how I did it, but I walked up to my brother's coffin with my mom. Seeing him lying there, looking as if he was asleep with his arms crossed over his chest destroyed something in me. Me and mommy were both bawling as we touched him, and I kissed his cheek. His skin felt weird. Dry. Cold. My heart shattered even more than it already had. I was so stricken with grief that I lost touch with reality for a moment. My mom was trying to lead me to our pew, but I resisted. I stared at my deceased brother, begging him to wake up. To please wake up! My father had to help mommy pull me away and sit with them.

I cried myself in a state of waking exhaustion and numbness. We left my brother in his final resting place and went to my grandmother's home for the repast. I sat on my nana's couch with my hands in my lap. Looking down at them as my family ate, drank, and spoke around me. My mom was next to me, talking to my aunt Crystal while daddy was out back with my uncles. Drinking and smoking. My grandma tried to get me to eat, but I couldn't. Avery dominated my mind. I saw his cute brown skinned face, that lopsided smile with his one dimple, I heard his laugh, and I just wanted to hug him again. Climb on his back again. Laugh my young heart out as he tickled me to death again. Once more, I started crying and got choked up. Mommy and aunt Crystal tried to comfort me, but I wanted someone else. I made my way through the dining room and kitchen, out the back door, and found my dad standing on nana's deck. The moment he saw me, he handed his beer to his brother Mark, came to me, picked me up, and carried me through the yard. With his back to the porch, I started bawling into my daddy's neck and he cried along with me.

****

The painful fire of Avery's death was beginning to calm when life threw gasoline on it. Bringing the flames of our agony roaring back. Within two months, both of the drug dealing thugs that shot it out in the park the day were caught. The first one was arrested three weeks after the shooting. He was identified by several people that were there that day. Cincinnati police apprehended him at his baby mamas' house. The next day, the second shooters face was on the news. His enemy gave him up to the cops. The detectives handling the case came by the house to inform my parents that they had officers searching the city for the second shooter, but the one they had in custody wasn't the one responsible for Avery's death. I was upstairs listening from the top of the stairs as the detective told my mother and father that the gun they recovered from the first suspect didn't match the bullet that killed my brother. Yet, that gun did kill one of the other boys. The focus now was finding the other shooter.

There was nothing for weeks on end. No sign of the man that killed my brother. Then, those same detectives showed up at our house again. I had just arrived home from school with my mom when they knocked on the door. They were there to deliver good news. The second shooter was in custody. He had fled Cincinnati after the shooting. Hiding in Detroit with a relative. That same cousin sold him out. By calling the local police to inform them that his wanted for murder cousin was laying low at his house. There was a cash reward for any information that led to his capture and he wanted that money. As the detectives spoke to me and my mom, Dontrelle Mason was in-transit from Michigan. Via the U.S. Marshall's that arrested him. Once he was turned over to them, he will be charged. Felony murder for my brother, attempted murder the other for the other boy he nearly killed. My mom hugged both detectives and they smiled at me as they promised that Avery and our family were going to receive the justice we deserved.

That was a promise that wasn't kept. The first shooter, Andre Phillips, was tried for killing a thirteen-year-old boy. He was found guilty and sentenced to life without the possibility of parole. Dontrelle Mason's case was far more complicated. His lawyers stalled the trial for months on end, he refused to take a plea bargain, and when he was finally in front of the judge and jury; my family and I thought we were going to get justice for the senseless death of my big brother. We didn't. Only two days into the trial, the judge had no choice but to dismiss the entire case. My people lost it in the courtroom that day. Dontrelle Mason walked on murdering my brother because of fucking technicality. I wish my parents hadn't brought me with them. One, I had to look at the piece of shit that killed my brother. Two, I was there to witness him smile and shake his lawyer's hand after the charges against him were dropped. The police and prosecution fucked up. Majorly!

The evidence numbers for the gun Dontrelle fired that day, the gun that killed Avery; were incorrect. The gun presented in court during the trial was the wrong one. Which that motherfuckers lawyer pointed out, the DA tried to fight it, but according to the law, the judge was left with no choice. Because positive identification of Dontrelle on the day of the shooting was weak and conflicted, plus the weapon presented by the prosecutor was not the gun matched to the bullet removed from my brother's body; the state had no case against Dontrelle Mason. All charges were dropped and he was free to go. That son of bitch murdered my brother and he got to walk Scott free. My mother cried into her hands as she was consoled by my grandma; my father and uncles cursed at judge and the man that killed Avery. I quietly sat there with my head down, tears trickling down my cheeks and dripping from my chin. My heart shattered all over again.

A month later, life continued to pour acid rain down on my family. I was at my grandmas' house with my mom. The Landon women were having a female only solidarity night. My mother, nana, and several of my aunts were seated around the dining room table drinking wine, talking, and playing cards. I was with my cousins in the living room. We had burgers, French fries, and other snacks while watching a movie. In the middle of everything, the house phone rang. My grandmother answered. Not twenty seconds after she listened to whomever she was speaking to told her something, she cried out, *"What??!!...Please, Jesus, No!!!"* All eyes were on nana as my mom rushed to her side and relieved her of the phone. I watched my momma's face change as she listened to whoever was on the other end deliver bad news. My mom's face went from shocked, to angry, to lost as she dropped the phone and stared at me across the dining room. As my grandmother cried in her arms, my mother shed silent tears as she revealed us what she and grandma just learned.

Daddy's rage over my brothers' murder got the best of him. We all seen and sensed it since Avery was killed. My brother was my dad's pride and joy. He loved us equally, but his son meant the world to him. He saw hope in Avery. He was raising his son to be one of high caliber. A leader, strong, smart, he was hard on him when it came to his education, never messing with the streets, excelling at sports, and always holding himself to a higher standard. My brother was ahead of his time and a bright future was waiting for him. Avery was going to be someone special. Even if he didn't make it to the NBA, he was going to be the example of the African-American dream. Young, black, gifted, positive, intelligent, and successful. Until a piece of shit, heartless drug dealing thug shot him in the stomach while trying to kill another equally worthless ass criminal. Over a girl they both were fuckin' and was playing them off of each other. My father had to bury his only son, live with the misery, then watch my brother's killer walk out of the courtroom on a technicality.

To come face to face with him less than two-months later. While we Landon females were having our solidarity night, my dad was with my uncles and a few of their friends at the bar. They were drinking beer and eating wings as they watched a pay-per-view boxing match. The story I learned later was that as my father was returning to his table from the bathroom. Just before the main event fight, Dontrelle Mason was sitting at a table with a couple of people. My dad proceeded to leave the bar, go to his car, grab his 9mm from the glove compartment, stroll back inside, walk up to the motherfucker that took his son from him, and return the favor. Daddy shot Dontrelle Mason four times. Killing him on the spot. It was my Uncle Rob that called my grandmother. My father never left the bar after he killed the man that murdered his boy. He sat down and began calmly smoking a cigarette and finishing his beer until the police arrived to arrest him. He was taken downtown, booked, and charged with First-Degree murder.

Months later, the charge was reduced to second degree homicide and my dad accepted a plea bargain. 12-to-24 years. The DA wanted to send my daddy away for life, but the judge intervened and showed my father a small bit of leniency. Still, on the day of his sentencing, when I was allowed to hug my dad, it took my mom, aunt, and grandma to pry my arms from around his neck. I was a mess that day. Crying and calling for my daddy as the court security officers took him away. When I finally stopped crying, I once again fell into a numbed state of silence. First, my brother was taken from me. Then life snatched my father away. I was half way through my ninth year on earth when depression and sadness wrapped their arms around me. Introducing themselves as my new best friends. At nine years old, I fell into a pit of isolation & suffering. I stopped talking, I didn't smile, I withdrew into myself, and my world became dark. I saw life in the ugly shades of black and white. Because the colors of beauty didn't exist for me anymore. My world was also cold, but I was being kept warm by a growing fire in me. The fire of anger.

****

Six months went by after my father was sent to state prison. Then nine months. A year. Eighteen months. A little over two-years after my dad was sentenced to a maximum of twenty-four years, my family was all but gone. A division developed between my mothers' side and my father's. For the first year of daddy's sentence, everyone was on board to support him. We all sent letters, visited him, I had mommy mail him copies of my report cards, money was put on his commissary account, and the family came together to hire a big shot black criminal defense attorney from Chicago to represent my father. In an attempt to get his sentence reduced. For more than a year, my father had all of us in his corner. Until members of the family on both sides changed up. Aunts, uncles, cousins, and friends of my dad began to pull back their support. They wrote him less, started skipping out on their visiting days, my mother questioned them about not accepting my dad's collect calls, and half of them stopped sending him money. Claiming to be broke, had priorities, or they made false promises to send daddy a couple of dollars "next week."

This kind of bullshit caused animosity and tension between my mother and fake ass, lying ass, so called family members. Animosity that sparked arguments and hostility. Which caused aunts, uncles, and cousins to fall back from my mother and I. My grandmother tried to keep us together, but my mom and members of the family that were abandoning my father decided to put their egos and emotions before my father. That lawyer from Chicago failed to get daddy's sentence reduced, there was no more money for another appeal, and during our annual joint family reunion; things only got worse. My mother and my dad's eldest sister got into a drunken verbal battle.

Before grandma could quell the fight and make peace, my mom and aunt declared war. It all began when mommy accused Aunt Charlene of turning her back on her brother. My auntie got mad and loud, as she always did when confronted about anything, causing nasty insults to be

16

flung back and forth. My mom ended up slapping the shit out of her sister-in-law. The altercation it spiraled into two grown women fighting like two possessed Hellcats in front of the entire family. In which family members from both sides decided to choose their own side. A one-on-one fight became an all-out riot level brawl in a public park.

No matter what my grandma did or said, she couldn't bridge the gap between the two sides of my family. Or, within the two sides. Blood had turned on blood. Most stopped talking to each other, they didn't socialize anymore, cousins were forbidden to hang out, there were sporadic fights, and the division only grew wider. It got so bad that my mom decided to move. She leased a smaller house in Columbus. We packed up and left Cincinnati. The only silver lining about the hour and a half move from home was that it put us closer to daddy. He was at Pickaway State prison. Which was now only half an hour away from us. Visiting my dad was the only thing that brought me out of my shell. I cried at the end of every visit, but I was still a daddy's girl. He made me smile, I enjoyed buying him snacks from the visiting room vending machines, I held his big hand the entire time, and we always took polaroid pictures. Life at home with my mom was cool, but I was always closer with my father. I wrote him every week, I looked forward to his calls on Tuesday and Sunday nights, and I still listened to and obeyed him from prison as if he was free.

I somewhat adjusted to life in a new city and attending a new school, but I was basically anti-social. I didn't make any new friends because I still had my bestie. Jamia. Her mom and mine were like sisters. Miss Sonja and my mother grew up together and she remained loyal to us. They visited us a lot and my best friend was the only one I needed. Though my heart still burned for Avery and my dad; the depression and sadness were starting to fade. I was going on eleven and really starting to emotionally breathe again when my mom filled my mental lungs with smoke. I began to notice signs that she was cheating on my dad at the same time her brother came to stay with us. Uncle Jeff was my moms' youngest brother at twenty-seven. He was one of those in and out of jail, corner boy hustling dudes that was always into some bullshit. My grandma persuaded my mom to be there for her brother by giving him a place to stay after he got out of prison. Uncle Jeff promised my mother that he wasn't going to be a problem. Swearing up & down that he was going to get a job, stay off the corners, and blah blah blah.

Uncle Jeffrey did get a job not long after he arrived in Columbus. In a barbershop. While in prison, he earned his barber's certification and a shop owner hired him. For a while, Uncle J was cool. He cut hair three, four days a week. Making decent money and he quickly made friends via the barbershop. My uncle was a talented barber and he was mad cute. Women were all over him and he was cool to be around. He was funny, I liked hanging out with him at home, and he was nice to me. I did catch on to the fact that my mom was seeing someone, but I couldn't bring myself to tell my dad. Thus, I pretended that I didn't know that my mother was fucking with another man as her husband did time. One night, mommy claimed that she was going out with a group of her co-workers. I was staying home with my uncle. Whom had to be paid to look after me so that I wasn't alone. Mommy went out to get her drink on, I suspected she was going to see her dude on the side, and I spent my Friday night in my room on the phone with Jamia as my Uncle Jeff played Xbox in the living room. On the phone himself.

I didn't know what time it was, but it was still dark when I was woken up. By my moms' brother. Uncle Jeff shook me awake, I opened my eyes, but before I could speak; he told me to be quiet. Aggressively. As he roughly pulled the cover off of me, I started to cry. He clamped his hand over my mouth, hissed at me to shut up, then started pulling my pajama pants off. As fear took over me, I cried, but I was frozen where I lied. My uncle stripped me nude from the waist down, then began touching me. With his hand over my mouth, I whimpered into his palm with my eyes squeezed shut. Once he was done with his fingers, he climbed on top of me, forced my legs open, and in the dimly lit darkness of my bedroom; pain became my entire reality. He never took his hand off my mouth as he tormented me. Uncle Jeff sounded like an animal as he pleased himself with my agony. I cried hard into his palm as tears squeezed through my shut eye lids. The pain was horrifying. I was screaming for it to end in my mind, I felt like I was going to throw up, and then he moaned out in sick, twisted satisfaction as he finished. Inside me.

I was shaking, terrified, in pain, and numb as my predator uncle cleaned up the evidence of his perversion. He made me strip my bed, he threw everything into the washing machine, and he forced me to take a shower. I was ordered to put on clean underwear and clothes, re-make my bed, and before he told me to go back to sleep; he threatened me. His threat scared me just as much as what he did to me. Once he left my bedroom, I crawled under my covers and bawled into my pillow. A few months shy of twelve and I was just raped by my uncle. I wanted my brother. I wanted my daddy. I wanted someone to come and take me away! I cried so hard that my body hurt. I wanted to tell my mom what Uncle J did, but his threat replayed over and over in my eleven-year-old mind. He promised that if I said a word about what happened, he'll kill my mom. Then, he'll kill me. The cold look in his eyes when he issued that threat told me that he was dead ass serious. I didn't want my mom to die, nor did I want to die. Thus, I wasn't going to say anything. To anyone about that night. I cried myself to sleep. In misery. Unaware of future nights like this.

The first of many to come.

CHAPTER TWO

*"Suffering is living in a body that fights to survive,
with a mind that wants to die."*

Before I was twelve-years-old I was only afraid of three things. The basement, Freddy Krueger, and my Uncle Jeff. After the night he crept into my bedroom and raped me, he was the only thing on earth that scared me. I so wanted to tell my mother what her brother did to me, but the fear of his threat to murder us forced me to keep that night to myself. Still, I thought that she would just notice. Notice that I was different. That I was more distant than normal. That I stayed in my room more often. Or that I wasn't interacting with my uncle anymore. Nor was he interacting with me. No. She didn't notice shit! My mother was far too busy feeling herself and doing her. It was now clear that she had herself a new nigga. All she did was work, go out, get her hair & nails done, and leave her daughter alone with her rapist! My uncle kept his distance from me, did his own thing, but when my mother was out at the bar or with her dude *(Whoever the fuck he was),* I banished myself to my room. With the door locked. Trying to forget, cope, and live with what he did to me.

On Friday and Saturday nights when my mom was out & about turning up, I was locked in my bedroom. Sitting on the edge of my bed, Indian style, blankly staring my TV screen as I played video games for hours on end. Pretending that I wasn't afraid. Afraid to leave my bedroom to get something to snack on. I began keeping junk food in my room. I was even too scared to go to the bathroom. Unless I knew that my uncle was asleep or not in the house. One night, I had to pee really bad. I had been holding it for a long time. Uncle Jeff was in the living room playing NBA2K as normal. I could hear his voice and laughter as he spoke to someone on the phone through his Blue-Tooth. It had been almost four months since the night he stole my virginity when he violated me. My bladder felt like it was about to burst when I said fuck it. I had to go. I exited my bedroom, walked down the hall, quickly entered the bathroom, and locked the door before dashing to the toilet. A few minutes later, as soon as I opened the bathroom door; there he was.

Uncle Jeff and I locked eyes for a second. His face was blank. As was mine. He didn't say anything to me as I lowered my head and he moved so that I could walk past him. I was trembling as I made my way back to my bedroom. Tears leaked from my eyes as I quickly locked my door and climbed onto my bed. With a framed photo of me and my dad. I curled up into a ball with it and cried onto the glass covering my daddy's face. I tried to block the memories of the night uncle Jeff raped me, but it was futile to even try. I remembered the pain, the sick feeling in my stomach, his savage grunts and moans, and the disgusting feeling of his semen. The more I thought about that night, the harder I cried. I cried so hard that it felt like I was suffocating. I cried myself to sleep for the hundredth time. However, unlike the previous ninety-nine times, I was sick and tired of just crying. It was time to get rid of my demon.

Eight days later. I was suddenly pulled out of class. By one of the guidance counselors. She escorted me to her office where I was met by my mother, principal, and a sex crimes detective from the Columbus Police. I sat next to my mom and the white male cop introduced himself. Detective Alex Winters. He was calm as he informed me that my father, from prison, had contacted his boss with an accusation. He claimed that I had written him a letter. Telling him that I was raped by my Uncle Jeffrey. It was dead silent for a while after the detective said that, then he asked me was it true? Was what I told my father true?

That I was sexually assaulted by my Uncle Jeffery? I looked at my mom before I answered. Though her eyes were enraged, she was crying. The counselor sitting on my opposite side was rubbing my back. Without looking at Detective Winters, staring at my mother, I told him yes. It was true. My uncle came into my room one night while my mom was out and he raped me. Tears slowly trickled down my cheeks as my mother and I held eyes. The detective gently asked me to look at him. When I gave him my attention, he had a pen and pad ready as he asked me to tell him what happened? Tell him everything. It was going to be had to revisit that night, but he needed to know it all. The detective encouraged me to be strong and gave me his word. What happened to me will not go unpunished.

I left school early that day. My mother, the counselor, and Detective Winters first took me to the hospital. We were met by a black female sex crimes cop who went in with me and my mom for my exam. They couldn't do a rape kit on me, but the doctor did "authenticate" that I had indeed engage in sexual intercourse. I heard her tell my mother and the lady cop that my hymen was broken and there were healed scars around my vaginal opening. My mom consented for them to draw my blood and swab me for testing. To see if I had contracted any STD's. I hadn't yet gone through puberty, so I hadn't had my first menstrual cycle; thus, they didn't even bother doing a pregnancy test on me. Once I was dressed again, I told my story again to black lady cop. Detective Yolanda Mitchell. When I was done, she stepped out of the exam room, returned five minutes later, and informed us that Detective Winters was on his way to pick up Uncle Jeff and we had to come with her to the precinct.

We left the hospital at 11:43 am. After nearly three hours at the police station with the detectives and a white lady from the prosecutor's office; we were allowed to go home. I went straight to my room and stayed there all night long. In the morning though, there was news from the police. They called my mother to tell her that her brother has been charged. They interrogated him for hours on end. Catching him in one lie after another until they wore his ass down and he caved in. He confessed to raping his eleven-year-old niece. My mom told me that they charged him with rape, statutory rape, molestation, and sexual assault of a minor. All in the first degree. As we sat at the dining room table, my uncle was locked away in the county prison. Without bail. My mother asked me why did I go to my father instead of her? I looked my mom right in the eyes and told her the truth. My father was the only parent I still trusted. Also, she was too busy living her best life to even notice how messed up I was and that she left me alone with Uncle Jeff in the first damn place! Then I got up from the table and went back to my room.

****

My uncle received the maximum penalty for raping me. He was done! He already had two strikes against him. When he was eighteen, he got hit with a three year stretch for dealing drugs. Then at twenty-two, he served another three-year sentence for assault. He caught his girlfriend at the time with another nigga and put the dude in the hospital. As a juvenile, starting at age ten, he was constantly arrested. In and out of detention, on probation twice, and a high school dropout delinquent. Instead of taking the deal to only serve eight to sixteen years; he hired a lawyer to fight the case. I had to look at my blood-related rapist in court as I told the jury what he did to me. My testimony, plus his confession *(which his attorney tried to claim was coerced)* sealed my uncle's fate. The jury deliberated for only two hours before they handed down their verdict. Guilty. On all of the charges. At his sentencing hearing, I looked my uncle in the face as I told him how much I hated him, reminded him of what he did to me, and I cried as I told him that I was happy that the jury found him guilty.

The judge showed uncle Jeff no mercy. He called him a monster and an incorrigible piece of subhuman garbage. Then, he imposed his sentence. My uncle actually started crying when the judge told him he was going to rot in prison for the rest of his natural life. 30-to-60 years. He then ordered the security officers to get him out of his damn courtroom! My life went on from the day my Uncle was escorted away in an orange jumpsuit and handcuffs. Though he went to prison, it didn't free me from the one my mind and heart were trapped in. The entire situation drove a rift between my mother and I. We often didn't speak to each other, I was old enough to not require someone to look after me, and my only break of sunshine through the gray clouds of my life was my father. Mom still took me see him twice a month, I wrote him all the time, and I spoke with him on the phone at least two times a week. I only had three constants in my world.

My daddy, silent isolation, and my best friend. Jamia was like the sister I never had. We were both seventh graders, but separated by over an hour of distance. At the Middle school I attended, shit was the same as when I arrived in Columbus. I was cool with a few people, but I didn't fuck with 99% of the student body. From day one, I kept to myself. All of my real friends were back in Cincinnati. Cliques and lifelong friends were already established when I moved to Columbus. Two things were clear. Not many were looking to make friends with me, nor was I eager to befriend anyone that didn't. Through it all, Miss Sonja and Jamia were consistent in my life. It was nothing new for my bestie to spend the weekend at our house or I stayed with them in Cincinnati. My best friend was the only person that knew how I truly felt. About Avery, the turmoil I lived with from being raped, the nightmares I had almost every night, and with her in my room listening to me and being there; I never felt alone.

It was with Jamia that I began to wild out. We both did. Her mom and mine were the same. Late 30's black women with teen daughters that didn't require around the clock supervision. My bestie & I were fourteen when we decided to act twenty-four. Our moms went out together a lot. Leaving us to have our own fun. No sooner than my mom and Miss Sonja left to bar hop or hit a club; Mia and I got our grown and sexy on. We changed into tight shirts & jeans, styled each other's hair, put on makeup, perfume, and went out to turn up. If I had known what was waiting for me on the path I chose to step on, I never would have. At the time, I was a confused teenager trying to run from her depression, sadness, and anger. I wallowed in that shit for months on end. The first time Jamia and I made our way to a park where the high schoolers kicked it, what I found there was just what I needed to heal myself.

Cigarettes, weed, liquor, and attractive male attention. At first, I was hesitant. After all, I was a rookie when it came to getting my party on. I had never smoked or drank anything before, nor had I flirted with niggas like that. I knew from school that I was on the radar with young dudes. The same as I was noticed by grown ass men outside of school. Before I was raped, and just after entering my teens; I was shy when it came to males. My father was hard on me and my mother about his daughter in society. As I got older, I came to understand why he felt that way. My body began developing around nine. By the time I was twelve, I was five foot three and half with popping out boobs, curves, hips, and far more butt than a pre-teen should have. Add in my light brown colored eyes, angel like-honey brown baby face, full-plump lips, and long dark brown hair.

I was an exact clone of my mom, grandma, and two of my aunts. Born pretty and beautifully built. By fourteen, I looked more like a young adult woman than a teenager. Five-six even, 135lbs, wearing a 34C bra with a big round bouncy ass. That's what all the boys at school talked about and what I caught men my fathers' age checking out when I walked down the street. It came to me in the months after my uncle was sent to prison. It was the way he acted when my mom was out. The way he looked at me, the way he always giving me compliments, being playful and touchie-feelie, and in the females he dated. They were all much younger than him. He was going on thirty, but every chick I saw him with was just barely on the adult side of eighteen. None older than twenty-one.

I didn't think much of it when it happened, but after he violated me, his behavior finally made sense. Those "accidental" brushes on my breasts or butt when we joked & played around, the way he stared at me for a second longer when he "accidentally" came into the bathroom as I was getting out of the shower, and it made me sick that he liked to take pictures of me on his phone. Playfully having me pose for him as we hung out in the living room while my mom was at the bar.

Jamia and I were night and day. She was smooth cocoa brown, I was a lighter shade of ebony. She had short hair, mine was several inches past my shoulders. I had the big butt, she had the big titties. I was five-six and athletic-thick, she was five-four and curvy-thick. Both of us were pushing fifteen, but by exterior alone, we could pass for nineteen or twenty. My bestie was far more social than I was, plus she was adventurous. When I told her that one of the chicks' I spoke to at my school had told me to come to the park on a Friday night to kick it; Mia was all for it. The first couple of times we chilled with the in-crowd, I didn't speak much, but I did indulge myself. I smoked my first cigarette, hit a blunt for the first time, and got my first taste of alcohol. Because I was a lightweight, those three hits of weed fucked me up. A small bit of Henny in a red cup accentuated my high and a Newport 100 accentuated my overall intoxication. I was loopy, smiling, acting silly with my bestie and a few other chicks, and I felt free. The pain that lived behind my eyes wasn't even relevant.

More and more as time went by, I embraced the wild side of life. I had to become two people. I didn't want to let my father down, so the Shanice I was in the daylight at school and around my mom was the one they recognized. My grades were good, I was still quiet, and I kept up the image of the girl my parents knew. When it was time to party and live it up; the other Shanice emerged. Once Jamia's mom or cousin dropped her off and my mom went out to do her thing with Miss Sonja or by herself; the good girl in me was left at home. My best friend and I met up with our little crew of home girls and niggas to live our best life. I was in high school now, still developing into a grown woman, and when not in the classroom learning; I was partying. I stayed high, drunk, I came to really enjoy freak dancing with niggas, dressing sexy, and I loved the attention that dudes smothered with. Niggas were on me. Twenty-four-seven.

I got hit on at school, going to or leaving, at the football & basketball games, at McDonald's, the mall, and especially at our little house parties and shit. I was a major flirt. I loved conversing with and teasing niggas, but I quickly became picky with the type of dudes I entertained. If a nigga was too short, fat, skinny, had nasty teeth, or dressed like a bum; I didn't even look at them, let alone give them the impression that I was interested. When a dude approached me, he had to have something going on. I didn't really care about money back then, but the motherfucker couldn't look like a pathetic ass clown. He had to be taller than me with a nice body, hair and teeth on point, dress style up to par, CLEAN

SNEAKERS, and he had to be attractive in my opinion. Sexy, cute, handsome; whatever. I had to be able to look at him, enjoy what I was saw, and envision myself kissing him. I learned that from Jamia. That's how she was and how I became. The only difference was that she wasn't shy about telling a nigga that he was a clown, a bum looking ass dude, corny, or ugly. Me on the other hand, I was a lot more subtle. More civil with my rejections, but I rejected an unworthy ass dude none the less.

****

I met my first boyfriend at a party one night. I was kicking with Jamia and our girls at this chick named Angie's house. Her people were gone for the weekend, so we decided to have ourselves a VIP only basement party. There was plenty of weed, beer, and liquor on deck. That night, I was feeling extra sexy. My father's only true friend did some real shit for my pops. My dad used to be in the drug game, but he got out when Avery was born. Then he was in and out until I was born. His best friend Dave was a lifelong criminal. He was locked up with my father and made him promise. That promise was kept when he was released nine months before. Ever since Dave got out, within a month, he started coming to Columbus to check on me and my mom. I knew that Uncle D gave my mother money to help out on my fathers' behalf, but she didn't know that before he would leave to head back to Cincinnati; he hit me off with some green backs too. Normally, he gave me like fifty bucks. That day though, he slipped me a thick wad of cash. $2,000 in twenties.

Before heading to the party, I took my best friend out and treated her right. We got our hair done, then our nails, and we hit up a connect for a new outfit. I was looking good in my new super tight black denim jeans, a form fitting white top, and a Black leather jacket that was sexy as fuck. All of it was Coogi. I got it from a girl that travelled all the way to New York City to boost clothing. Jamia was rocking Gucci and she looked sexy as Hell too. It was around 11:00 pm when my bestie and I were sitting next to each other near the back of the basement. Both of us had a cup of Henny and I was smoking a cigarette as we conversed while marinating our high. The music was flowing, everybody was chilling, and I happened to look up and see him as he entered the basement. Through the THC cloud in my brain and the liquor flowing through my veins, I stared at him as if I was incapable of looking away.

I watched him like a hawk as he dapped niggas fists, half hugged others, and fully hugged chicks as he made his way through the

26

basement. I didn't know him, never seen him before, and had no idea what his name was; but none of that mattered right then. I was liking what I was seeing. I assessed that he was about six-foot-one with a very nice build, dark brown skinned, and he had all the right characteristics. Short flowing waved hair with a sharp line up and fade, his beard was squared & trimmed, he had high cheek bones, full-juicy lips, and his outfit was on point. Dude was rocking Mitchell & Ness Cleveland Indians varsity jacket, a crisp white T, baggy dark blue denim jeans, and brand new looking white-on-white Nike Air Force One's. Around his neck was long silvery chain with a matching watch on his wrist. My eyes followed him as he acquired himself a red plastic cup of E&J before joining a cipher of three niggas not too far away as they shared a blunt.

I was in and out of the conversation with my best friend as I eye stalked Mr. Sexy as he got lit. I smoked my Newport, taking sips of my Henny as I watched him laugh, joke, and rap with his niggas. As I sat there unable to take my eyes off of him, I felt myself getting turned on. In my opinion, he was beautiful as a motherfucker. I liked everything I saw about him. He had me biting my lip and breathing a little harder than normal. Then, he caught me staring at him. Our eyes locked and my chest started heaving a bit as he grinned at me while approaching with his red cup in hand. I stared at him as he walked over, took the empty chair next to me, and with his face close to mine; he introduced himself. Raheem. We shook hands, I told him my name, he kept his eyes locked with my own, and we just started talking. About twenty minutes later, I ended up outside with him on Angie's back porch. Raheem and I flirted as we sipped from our red cups. He had me on fire. His physical nature, the sound of his voice, the way he looked at me, and the vibe he was giving off.

I thought he was like twenty, twenty-one, maybe twenty-two-years old. The way he looked and carried himself was more of a grown man. Then Raheem revealed that he just turned eighteen a month before. That meant he was a little over three-years older than me. My fifteenth birthday was in a month and a half. Though he was legally an adult, I didn't give a fuck. This nigga had me in his web. I was crushing on him. Hard! So much in fact, that when he asked me was I cool with leaving the party to kick it with him, I didn't hesitate to say yes. I informed Jamia that I was out, told where I was going, and Angie chimed in to say that Mia was cool with her. She can crash in her room. I hugged my bestie and left with Raheem. He even had his own car. A sleek midnight blue Lexus ES300. We drove to a diner, talked more over food, and then drove around the city for a while. Getting to know each other. It didn't take me long to figure out what Raheem was. A drug dealer. A hustler that drove with a gun in his lap, constantly watched his rear-view mirror, and though he was laid back; I sensed that he was a violent individual.

Knowing what he was only turned me on more. A sexy as fuck drug dealing thug. It was my lucky night in my mind. Raheem took me to where he stayed. A row house on the eastside of town. His sister and her two kids lived there too, but they weren't awake when we arrived. He led me to his bedroom, then closed and locked the door. I knew that he wanted to fuck from the moment we met. Strangely, I was ok with that. I was doing me. If this sexy motherfucker wanted some pussy, I was going to give it to him. Niggas had been on my ass for long time and I never gave it up. There was something about Raheem that made loosen my reserve and just go with the flow. We got right to it from the moment he locked the door. He first put on some music. On the TV. A hip-hop music channel. He turned the lights off and the room was now lit by the TV screen. I sat on the edge of his King-sized bed and began taking my jacket off. Staring up at him as he removed his. Though I was nervous, I didn't show it. Something in me wanted this.

Raheem and I were both naked now. I was lying on my back, he was on top of me, and I caressed his back as he kissed me. Mmmmmm! I loved how he tasted. His juicy lips were warm. He made me wrap my legs around his waist as his tongue slid into my mouth. With my eyes closed, I moaned into him as his big dick was pressed against my belly; trapped in between us. I didn't know if it was the fact that I was drunk and high, but the heat of Raheem's body felt so damn good. By the time he moved his lips to my neck, I wasn't nervous anymore. I was hypnotized by that good feeling. I couldn't stop moaning or open my eyes as he moved down my body. I bit into my lip and arched my back, clutching his head as he began sucking on the nipple of my left titty. I opened my eyes a little as he moved to the right one. Doing the same thing he did to the left. Sucking on and licking my nipple until it was hard as a marble. After pleasing my breasts, he moved further down my torso.

I propped myself up on my elbows as Raheem opened my legs as he pushed them up. My breathing increased as I watched him move his face to my pussy. The moment his fingers spread my pussy lips and his tongue made contact with my clit; my head dropped back. I closed my eyes and opened my mouth. As the tip of his tongue rotated in a slow circle on my clitoris, each rotation sent shocks of pleasure through my entire body. I moved my hips in a circle, following the motion of his tongue as I moaned. Raheem ate my pussy for a long ass time. Making me moan louder and harder; almost louder than the rap songs playing in the background. He started fingering me with two fingers as he feasted on my clit. He had me shaking, sucking in air, looking down at the top of his head, biting my lip, and nearly crying from how good it felt to get my pussy eaten. Then, it happened. My first orgasm. I was gone. Losing control of my body, mind, and reality.

All I felt was electricity, heat, a vibration, and tightness. Raheem fought with my legs as I shook and convulsed. My upper body twisted to the side and I was moaning hard and painfully with my eyes tightly squeezed shut. When my first orgasm finally receded, I could see and hear again. My body was still trembling as Raheem kept fingering me. No longer eating me out as his deep voice marveled at what was happening. He was like, *"Damn you get wet when u cum!"* Then, he excitedly told me that he had to fuck this pussy. Raw. I watched him climb on top of me as I grinned through half open eyes. Opening my legs for him. I lifted my head as he positioned himself. Watching as he guided his dick towards my pussy. I didn't know how he big it was, but it had to be at least eight-inches long and thick. The head was huge. I learned all about a nigga with a big dick when Raheem penetrated me. Pleasure went away with Pain's arrival. Wet pussy or not, his penis hurt like a motherfucker when he put it in.

My eyes slammed shut, I turned my head to the side, bit into my bottom lip, moaned in pain, and gripped Raheem's arms as he filled my pussy. His dick felt good, but it hurt as it stretched me out. He was in Heaven though. Groaning like Pit Bull as he started stroking. His vice dripped with ecstasy as he told me how tight my pussy was. How juicy wet it was. He gripped my hair as he increased both the depth and force of his strokes. I moaned hard with each thrust. Trying to enjoy the sex through the pain. When I opened my eyes, a tear fell from each one. I stared at the door of Raheem's closet as stroked back and forth inside me. Out of nowhere, memories of the night my uncle raped me began flashing in my mind. The flow of my tears increased and with Raheem fisting my hair and now stroking hard; for a moment, I wasn't there. I felt everything though. The painful ramming of his dick in my vagina, his hard grunts of satisfaction, my own heartbeat, the heat of his body, and the turmoil in my soul.

I almost made Raheem stop and get the Hell off me when my own body intervened. I clutched him, digging my nails into his skin. With my eyes closed, I opened my mouth. Wide. I was cumming again. This was one was stronger than the first one and I felt more pleasure than pain this time. Raheem was going hard and fast inside me. My wetness merged with the music. He was sweating and moaning his damn self. His dick felt good now. Real good. Like a euphoric drug; I just wanted more. And more. Over the Jay-Z song playing on the TV, I could hear the squishing wetness of my pussy with each thrust of his penis. Raheem was going all in now. He rammed his dick back and forth in me. I kept my head to the side, eyes, closed, smile on my face, loving the hot jolts of pleasure waving through my body as he announced that he was cummin'. Moments later, I felt him pull his dick out. Then I felt his warm semen shooting onto my belly and all over my titties. That felt good too. He was out of breath, I was riding a cloud, we finally cleaned up, I put on his white T, and we went to sleep.

Raheem and I smoked a cigarette before lying down. He left the TV on and as I lied on my side with my back to his chest and his dick against my butt through his boxers; I channel surfed. While embracing everything that I felt. Pleased, warm, safe, comfortable, and at ease. I liked Raheem more than I did at the party when I first saw him. It really felt like he was into me too. Being close to him, kissing him, fucking him, and now sleeping next to him felt like life. His presence was giving me the two things that were missing ever since my daddy was sent to prison. Feeling special and a sense of security. I haven't even known Raheem for twenty-four hours, but we had sex and I felt close to him. I snuggled in his embrace as I yawned. Yes. I felt very close to this dude. I loved how my body felt against his, he was sexy as Hell, and our first-time fucking was nothing but pure fire. Most importantly, I felt safe with him. Next to him. I fell asleep not caring about anything else in the world.

Except for this good feeling that I never wanted to lose.

CHAPTER THREE

"I'm with some hood girls lookin' back at it,
And a good girl in my tax bracket,
Got a Black card that'll let Saks have it,
These Chanel bags is a bad habit."

-Nicki Minaj, Feeling myself

At only 17-years old, I felt like the baddest bitch in Columbus. I was five-seven and a half, an even 140lbs, and my curves were sharper than a razor's edge. My face matured to a woman's image, my hair & nails were always on point, and I was living my best life. Though I dropped out of high school, I didn't require a diploma to make it in this world. Shit! I had more money in my pocket and was living a far more luxurious life than most chicks that had jobs. My man was a consistent money-making hustler. Raheem sold coke and weed like he manufactured the shit himself. Being that I was his girl and I played my part as the ride or die chick he shaped me to be; I cruised on the highway of life in the easy lane. For like the first six months we were together, our relationship was subtle. I was still in school and living at home while he did his thing on the streets. Every weekend though, I was with him. We spent most of our time at his house, but more often than not he took me a hotel. Where I gave myself to him. Any way he wanted me.

Raheem had a high sex drive and I catered to his every need. We fucked all the time. At night, in the morning, late afternoons; whenever. Friday and Saturday nights were the highlights of my week. More and more as I got older, my mom seemed less and less concerned about me. We didn't really see a lot of each other during the school-work week to begin with. Monday to Thursday, in the evenings, it was the same routine. One of us cooked dinner or we ordered something; we ate in the living room while watching TV; then both of us did our own thing. Me in my room doing my homework with my music bumpin', my mom at the dining room table with her bottle of wine, menthol Kool's, and on the phone with whoever. Laughing and talking about old school shit. School came to be boring to me, but I kept at it for my daddy. I maintained good grades so that when I mailed him my report cards, he would be proud of me. Far as I knew, I was the only person on earth besides his homie

Dave that was still loyal to him. His approval and love meant the world to me. Thus, no matter what, I did what I could to make him proud.

The other man I sought to please was my boyfriend. Raheem and I weren't all out in the open with our relationship. His people knew, but because he was the bread winning drug dealer that supported his sister and her kids, plus other family members; none of them saw a problem with him dating a fifteen-year-old when he was going on nineteen. For a while, what we had was based on two things. Sex and money. Raheem gave me plenty of both. It was with him that I developed my freaky side. Especially when it came to giving head. My man loved, absolutely loved to get his dick sucked. His was the first I put my mouth on and he taught me how to do it right. How to lick it properly, stroke it, massage his sack, deep throat, use my lips to make love to it, apply lots of saliva, and though it took a while; I came to like swallowing his cum. Once I knew how to suck a dick like a pro, I loved doing it as much as he loved getting it. Giving my man head became a norm for me. I sucked his dick early in the morning, in the shower, while he was watching a game, even as he was driving. I became addicted to feeling his big dick in my mouth that I got wet sucking it.

When it came to fucking, I craved Raheem in my pussy as much I did my mouth. I was scared of getting pregnant for a while because we never used condoms. Though he pulled out, a few times he busted a nut inside me. Jamia had the same concern about getting knocked up, so my best friend and I went on birth control at the same time. We got our pills at the free clinic downtown, but she decided to be extra careful. She grabbed a big handful of condoms from the jar in the lobby as we left. I thought about grabbing some too, but decided that I didn't need any rubbers. I was only fucking one dude. Jamia messed with multiple niggas. She wasn't the boyfriend type of chick. My best friend was a stick & move girl. Once I was on the pill, Raheem still pulled out to bust all over me, but he came in me more often now that we didn't have the fear of having a baby. That was fine by me. I loved the feeling of his warm cum in my pussy anyway.

We were coming up on six months together when my home life took a bad turn. My mother was on some real bullshit. First; she filed for divorce from my father. Second; she flaunted her new nigga in my face. Dude started coming to the house to spend time with her. Even when I was home. Third; she cut my dad off completely. She still took me to visit him, but she didn't want to see him anymore. Because I was a minor, she had to accompany me to the prison. Yet, she didn't go into the actual visiting room with me. She signed us in, but remained out in the waiting area while I went in to spend time with my daddy. He didn't say anything, but I could see it in his eyes. His wife left him high and dry. Abandoned him. All he had left was me. As the months and years rolled by, watching my father rapidly age from the stress & misery of no longer having a family angered me something fierce. He advised me to not harbor hate towards my mom, but that was impossible not to do.

The silence and distance between her and I only deepened as I moved towards sixteen-years old. Every time I saw her, I cut my eyes at her. When her man Jerome would come over, I would leave. I didn't want to see her all lovey dovey with him or hear them fucking behind the closed door of her bedroom. To add insult to injury, my mother tried to get me to embrace and interact with her nigga. Sit down to dinner with them and she invited me to accompany them to the movies and shit. No thank you was my answer. Each and every time she offered. Things came to a head one evening when I came in from shopping at the mall. My mom and Jerome were sitting close together on the couch. Drinking wine and watching a movie. I planned on just going to my room, putting my things away, taking a shower, smoking a blunt, and talking to Jamia on the phone until I went to bed. Only my mom decided to pretend that she and I were cool.

By asking me what did I get at the mall. To show her. I ignored her as I headed for the stairs. She asked me again what I bought at the mall, but with an attitude this time. I stopped at the bottom of the stairs, looked at her, glanced at Jerome, and made the decision to keep it 100 with what was on my mind. I informed my mom that she and I weren't cool. She was my mother, I was her daughter, she had her life, I had mine, and I wanted no parts of her goddamn soap opera! There was a silence as we stared at one another, then she gave Jerome her wine glass, rose up from the couch, and began cussing me out as she approached me. Loudly inquiring as to who in the entire fuck was I talking to like that?! That I must have lost my motherfuckin' mind to have the audacity to speak to her as I just did. I said nothing as she walked up on me. Due to us being the same height, we were eye level as she went on a tirade about respecting her in her fucking house, who did I think I was, that she paid all the bills and rent in this bitch, and if I ever spoke to her like that again she was going to put her motherfuckin' hands on me!! I looked my mom up and down, licked my lips, nodded my head, then dropped my bags.

The police arrived twenty minutes later after a neighbor called them. Two patrolmen knocked on the door, Jerome let them in, and they found me and my mother looking like we got jumped. Our hair was fucked up, clothes were torn a bit, and we both had a few scratches and bruises. They spoke to us in separate rooms and neither of us lied. My mom and I went at it like two pit bulls. The inevitable mother-teen daughter fist fight after a long time of silent hostility. The patrol officers spoke privately on the porch, called someone, then came back in and asked us did either of us want to press charges against the other? I said no, as did my mom. She told the officers that the entire incident was an argument that got out of control and that it won't happen again. The cops let us off with a warning and then left. Once they were gone, my mother grabbed me by my arm, escorted me into the kitchen, roughly released me, and then banished me from her life like she did my father.

I was told to pack my shit and get the fuck out of her house. That when she woke up in the morning; I better be gone. If I was still here when she got up, she was calling Children and Youth services to have me declared a delinquent. Then, I'll be removed by them and placed into system. My mom looked me in my eyes as she told me that since I thought I was grown and had the audacity to swing on her, then it was time for me to go. I was no longer welcome in her home, or in her life. She got in my face and told me to never come back, she didn't ever want to see me again, and that I was no longer her daughter. I was a fuckin' stranger to her now! Then she turned and walked out of the kitchen, reminding me of the threat she made. I had until morning to figure out where I was going. No sooner than she and Jerome made their way up to her bedroom, I started for mine. The first thing I did was call Jamia. I told her what happened, we talked about what I was going to do, and then I informed her that I will call her back. I then called Raheem. After I told him what happened, he informed me to get my shit ready. He'll be there to get me in an hour.

****

I thought my man was going to move me into his house with him and his sister. That's where we went the night he picked me up, but I was only there for a week before he set up a better option for me. A one-bedroom efficiency apartment that was six-blocks from my high school. The spot was pretty big, already furnished, and only cost $350 a month. Raheem turned on the utilities, bought me a TV and shit, and paid the rent for six months. As we were setting my new place up, he explained to me why I couldn't live with him. He didn't want friction between me and his sister, he was only at the row house when he had to be, and because of how deep in the streets he was; he had no central address. The same as he had no registered cell phone, car, bank account, or any internet presence. He was serious about his business and was trying to have nothing that traced back to him. He told me not to worry about the rent because he got that covered. Yet, he informed that since I was still in high school but on my own now, I was going to have to learn some shit and do for myself.

I went from a sixteen-year-old high school girl that lived at home, to a Junior that lived on her own and sold weed for her man. Mad people in my age group smoked, so I pushed bags of chronic for Raheem to them. Every weekend while he was spending time with me at my spot, before he left Sunday night, I was given my package for the week. $700 worth of weed. Raheem taught me how to break the buds down and bag up. I sold nicks, dimes, twenties, and quarters. Rah's connect supplied him with high-grade bud. I always sold out by Friday. Out of $700, my take was $300. That was my life for quite a while. I went to school, sold weed, chilled at home, and spent time with my dude. I was stacking money week in and week out. Treating myself well and enjoying my life. Jamia still came by to kick it with me. We had more fun than ever being that I had my own place & money. However, our paths in life were going in different directions. My plan was to drop out of school. Hers was to keep going.

I signed out of high school in the eleventh grade. My best friend was working towards graduating and heading off to college. Jamia and I were the same, yet different. She was just as party hard, promiscuous, and hood as me; but she had something that I lacked. Goals. Ambitions. Dreams. My bestie wanted to earn a college degree and achieving positive success. Her focus was on establishing her own business; mine was being catered to. Still, my best friend had my back. She didn't judge me and was always there for me. Raheem had no objections to my dropping out of high school. He stepped things up though.

He now hit me off with $1,500 worth of weed to sell each week. My cut was now $500 and he schooled me even further. My man taught me how to drive and he moved me into a bigger & better apartment. As I turned seventeen and he celebrated his twentieth birthday; Raheem motivated me to progress more into a woman. At his advice I started to going to the gym, I had a standing reservation with a hair & nail stylist, and he frequently took me on shopping trips. I was closing in on the end of my time as a juvenile, but I looked and carried myself like a grown ass woman.

Life was sweet until a few months after my eighteenth birthday. My world was simple. My days were spent doing me. I had a routine. I hit the gym to work out in the morning, dropped by the salon, I ate well, shopped, and rolled around Columbus in my ride. Raheem bought me a dark blue Nissan Altima after I got my license. Though my car was pre-owned, it was damn near new, clean, and he put in a banging sound system and smoke tints. It was in my name and he gave me the money to make the monthly payments. In between everything that I did during the day, I made my drops. When someone wanted some smoke, they hit my phone. In text, they entered a code for how much they needed and where they were. I made the delivery, got paid, and bounced. Just like that. Raheem schooled me to keep it to business. Drop and move. That's exactly what I did. Other than that, I kept to myself. I didn't fuck with anyone really. Besides Jamia, I didn't have any home girls. That was cool with me. My life was exactly the way I wanted it to be.

I was never really the type of chick that needed to be around a bunch of bitches anyway. All that catty, jealous, bitter, petty, and backstabbing shit wasn't for me. The older I got, the more I saw most females for what they were. Two-faced, hating ass bitches. Chicks that didn't even know me acted like I did something foul to them. At the salon, because I was dipped in the finest shit and had a fat wad of cash; I got the looks. The evil side eyes, envious glances, expressions like I stank, and that up & down look as if I wasn't shit. Because I had the nerve to look good in name brand clothing and footwear. Chicks with knockoff outfits, no car, and very little money to their name hated on me because we weren't on the same level. Not my fault or my damn concern. Appearances didn't even matter. I received the envious, I HATE YOU look from pretty, ugly, fat, and nicely built bitches alike. Women who looked as if they had some dough and from busted-broke chicks just the same. That's why I liked the fact that I was a loner. I didn't have the tolerance for the dumb shit.

Just when I thought happiness and comfort in my world would remain as it's been; life kicked me square in the teeth. Jamia was half way across the country. She decided to attend an HBCU to further her education. My home girl earned herself a full-ride scholarship to Howard University in Washington D.C. I was happy for her and we spoke on the phone often as she settled into the flow of her first semester. However, the more she had to focus on her studies and classes; the less we talked. My bestie tried to keep our line of communication consistent, but when she started calling less and the time of her responses to my texts and emails got longer and longer; I let her be. Falling back so that she could do her thing at school. Raheem was doing big things on the streets of Columbus and outside the city. My man was stacking money and making major moves. People were talking about him on the streets as if he was a Kingpin. He was going on twenty-one-years old. To be so young, he handled business like a hustling mastermind. I heard all the rumors, whispers, and stories about the violent side of what he did. I didn't care though.

That man loved me. Hard. He took care of me, catered to all my needs, pampered me, respected me, and satisfied me in all ways. By the time I turned eighteen, it wasn't even about the money and shit. I loved him with all that I had and treated him like a King. Long before my mother turned her back on my dad, I watched her treat him as if he was royalty. Growing up, I watched my father come home from work to a woman that loved him, fed him, washed his dirty clothes, got his uniform ready for work in the morning, and catered to him when he was watching football or something. That's exactly how I was with Raheem. I cooked for him, did his laundry, massaged his back as he slept, kept my body right for him, gave him all the pussy he desired, and relieved his stress from the streets by sucking his dick without him asking me to do it. The hood may have known him as a drug dealer that wasn't shy about pulling his gun; but to me, he was mine. My King. The love of my life. I never questioned my safety or happiness with him. Rah was my world.

I saw the storm coming, but was far too comfortable and unable to see the future to know how destructive it was going to be once it hit. It was a normal day for me when it all went down. I was in the middle of getting a manicure and new style when I overheard two chicks talking about my man. I was about to get mad and check their asses when one of them said something that forced to pay closer attention to their conversation. I watched the stylist work on my nails as one of the chicks behind me said to her friend that she heard from her baby dad sister that the police and Feds was all over the northside. They were locking down corners, arresting niggas, raiding trap houses, and that they heard Raheem got popped too. The second I heard that, I no longer gave a fuck about my nails. I stopped the technician, tossed her fifty bucks, grabbed my purse and was out the door. After I pulled off from the nail shop, I took out my phone and tried to call Raheem. With my heart pounding in my chest. His phone went to voice mail. Three times. I was starting to shake as I hit his number for a fourth time. It was ringing again when I was interrupted.

By an unmarked police sedan's lights and sirens behind me. I pulled over a block later. With both of my hands on the steering wheel like Raheem taught me, I watched a regular police cruiser roll to a stop in front of me as two plainclothes detectives approached my car from the rear. Two patrol officers and two narcs surrounded my car. Hands on their holstered guns. The detective outside my door ordered me to roll my window down. I did as he instructed. He then told me to shut my engine off, remove the key from the ignition, and slowly drop it out of the window. Once again, I complied. The cop took a step back, kept his hand on his Glock holstered on his hip, then ordered me to step out of my vehicle. Keeping my hands in sight. No sooner than I exited my car, I was ordered to turn around and put my hands on my head. Fingers interlaced. I offered no resistance as I was patted down, handcuffed, and escorted to the unmarked sedan. The cop explained to me that I was being taken in for questioning in regards to my boyfriends' criminal activities.

****

The police weren't the ones that questioned me at the precinct. I sat in an interrogation room for over an hour until this white woman in a sharp pants suit strolled in. She was tall and blond with bright blue eyes and a snake like smile. She identified herself as ADA Melissa Forbes. A senior prosecutor from the Narcotics Division of the District Attorney's office. I said nothing. I just stared at her. Before she questioned me, she gave it to me straight. Raheem was in custody. He was being charged with both federal and state level narcotics possession, distribution, illegal weapons, etc, etc. ADA Forbes gave me the blue-eyed stare with her devil grin as she informed me that my man has been under investigation-surveillance for more than six months and they basically had everything they needed to bury him, his associates, and his connection. That evil ass smirk on her arrogant face widened as she explained that she knew from surveillance that I was his girlfriend. That she knew, that I knew, that he was major drug dealer in Columbus. She rattled off my address, my daily habits, who my mother was, and that it was in my file that my father was serving time for murder.

This prosecutor bitch then offered me what she called a golden ticket. She cocked her head as she expressed that they didn't want me. Far as she was concerned, I was simply the girlfriend of a drug dealer. That in itself wasn't a crime. Forbes then lowered her voice as she offered me a deal. She was willing to let me walk if I helped her out. If I agreed to cooperate. By signing a sworn statement detailing Raheem's involvement in drug trafficking. The ADA told me that if I agreed to become a confidential-cooperating witness, no charges will be levied against me. However, if I refused, then she will have no choice but to drop a Felony II charge of criminal conspiracy on me. Before I could respond, she told me that I had twenty minutes to decide. In mean time, could she get me anything to help make my decision. A cigarette, I dryly replied. A few minutes after the ADA exited the interview room, a detective came in with a half pack of Newport shorts, a book of matches, and a small metal ashtray.

Two and a half cigarettes later, ADA Forbes returned for my decision. She sat down, stared at me for a moment, then asked what was my choice? I took one more drag on my cig, stubbed it out while holding her stare, and gave her my answer. Half an hour later. I was fingerprinted, had my mug shot taken, I answered a bunch of personal questions for a female patrol officer, then I was transported to the county jail. My reality for the next year. I was charged with three counts of conspiracy, but the lawyer I hired got two of the charges dropped. I accepted a plea bargain on one count of criminal conspiracy charge and was sentenced to twelve months county time. It was true. The state didn't want me. I wasn't important to their case, but I refused to be their puppet against my man. Thus, they railroaded me with a bullshit charge. A charge I had to serve a year in prison for.

During which everything that I loved and treasured was stripped from me.

PART TWO
COLD HEART

*"People say that I'm fucked up,
but I won't apologize for anything that I do.
The same way life and society doesn't apologize
for making me this way."*

CHAPTER FOUR

"No one gives it to you…You have to take it."

-Frank Costello, The Departed

By the time I went before the judge after agreeing to plead guilty; I had been down for four months. I only had eight more months to serve. Even though I was charged with conspiracy and didn't have a criminal record; the arraignment judge revoked bail. The prosecutor persuaded him to reject any type of bond by convincing him that I was a flight risk. Those first four months went by slow as fuck. Life in the county was on a fixed routine. There was nothing to do other than watch TV in the dayroom, sleep, play cards, or read books. Out of my first one-hundred and twenty-two days in prison; I spent forty-five of them in solitary confinement. Bitches on the street were bad enough, but chicks in jail were even worse. I got into several fights in Gen-pop that landed me in the hole. Three times. My first trip was seven days, #2 was for ten days, and my third visit down to the restricted housing unit was for twenty-five days of total isolation in a small cell. After my third visit to the hole, I was transferred to the segregation block. Protective & administrative custody.

For the last eight months of my sentence, I cut myself off from the world around me. I had a cell by myself, I read most of the day, worked out in my cell, didn't speak to anyone at chow time, and kept my distance. I had to come to terms with something that hurt me to my core. Raheem was sentenced to thirty-five years. He too refused to cooperate with the law. He gave them nothing. Accepting his fate with a federal jury. I asked my lawyer to look into my man's case and he did just that. My boo was gone. I had no idea which federal prison they were sending him and it was reality that I was never going to see him again. I cried a lot because it took a while for the memories of us to fade away. I thought about calling my mother to come see me, but decided not to. We haven't spoken to or seen one another in a long time. There was no use bridging that gap now. She said that she never wanted to see me again, so I kept that going. I didn't really want to see her either. Then, there was my father. He was gone too.

At the start of my seventh month in the county, a guard came to my cell to get me. She escorted me to one of the counselor's offices' in the main building. The counselor offered me a seat before informing me that she was contacted by the Ohio Department of Corrections. She regretted to inform me that my father has passed. He died a few days before after being rushed to a civilian hospital following a massive stroke. I tried to maintain a hard exterior, but tears bust loose from my eyes as I lowered my head. The counselor was supportive and comforting, allowing me some time to cry and grieve in her office before I was returned to my cell block. My dad's sister claimed his body, took him back to Cincinnati, they laid him to rest, and one of my cousins was nice enough to mail me the program from his funeral. Because my request to attend was denied. For days on end, I barely left my cell. I rarely was out of my bunk either. I had a little radio from commissary, so when I wasn't lying there listening to music, I was asleep. Or I cried myself to sleep.

One year went by. I was two months past nineteen and my time in prison was over. I turned in my two-piece khaki uniform, gave away all my shit, a guard escorted me to processing, and I changed into the clothes I was wearing when I arrived twelve months before. Minutes after signing out in reception, I walked out of prison. It was a good thing I had some cash in my wallet when I was sent to the county. Because my ATM card had expired. My account still had some money in it though. $5,387.98 plus the $350 in cash in my purse. That was all I had to my name. I caught a city bus a few blocks from the jail and got off near the shopping district. Before I bought some clothes that fit and set up a place to stay for the time being; I satisfied my craving and a need. I bought a pack of Newports and hit up Burger King. After that, I went into an urban fashion store and bought a load of low-cost clothing and footwear to hold me over for a while, then I found myself a place to live until I made something better happen.

A thousand bucks to a perverted looking older black dude established a roof over my head. In a cheap one level motel. I had the option of paying by the day, week, or month. I made the decision to pay enough that I didn't have to worry about a place to live for the time being. My room was much bigger than my cell. It came with a color TV, a small fridge, a double bed, and after a year of shitting three feet from where I slept; I had a real bathroom. I took a long hot shower, shampooed / conditioned my hair, threw on a pair of shorts and a tank top, then spent the rest of the day chilling. I watched TV, smoked, dinner consisted of pizza & wings, I got a bottle of Henny from a wine & spirits two blocks away, then I went to bed. Alone and full of drive, anger, sadness, and hate. I did my year in prison, lost the love of my life, my apartment, car, the money I had saved, and my daddy was resting in peace back in Cincinnati next to Avery. My mother and I were estranged, my best friend was away in college, and I didn't fuck with either side of my family. I was utterly on my own. No friends, no support, and nothing but me, myself, and fuckin' I to figure shit out.

I was released from the county as a nineteen-year-old high school drop out with a felony on my record and no work experience. I had a year to think on what I was going to do once I was released. I knew a bit about the drug game from my time with Raheem, but I didn't want to be a dealer. I could do it, but I saw more risks than rewards. The same went for armed robbery. I couldn't see myself doing it. After weeks of brain storming in my cell, it dawned on me that I was born with all the assets I required. I was pretty, my body was right, I knew how to dress, and my sexual forte was fire. Four factors that most men are weak about. Men in general, thirsty men in particular, and thirsty men with money specifically. That was my plan. Play niggas for money. A day and a half after being released from the county; I was on a mission. I dipped into my cash and got myself right. I took care of my hair, nails, bought two pre-paid phones, purchased a couple sexy looking outfits and shoes from the mall, then went back to my motel and got ready.

It was a Thursday night and I started my bar hopping quest at eight pm. For a little more than an hour, I entertained conversation with only two types of men. Niggas that looked like hustlers and older niggas that had that sugar daddy feel to them. Dudes with a broke vibe, or I GOT A WIFE AT HOME looking niggas were ignored and rejected before they could waste even a second of my time. I left the first bar at 9:25 with three phone numbers. Two were mid-to-late twenties hustling niggas and the third was a forty-nine-year-old that had pension and benefits written all over him. I took a cab to another bar close to where I used to live. This spot was known for deep pockets and the ghetto fabulous. I was in there for close to two and half hours. Niggas were eager to buy me drinks. I was pressed up on me the entire time I was there. I flirted with one dude after another. Damn near behaving like a cat in heat. I had five niggas in the palm of my hand and one wanted to fuck that night. He was drooling to take me to hotel. I left him with a hard dick in his pants and his number in my phone.

After two days of non-stop texting, sending nude pics, and phone sex; it was time to get paid. I had more than a dozen niggas in my phone and I told each one the same thing. They had to pay to play. My time nor my body was free. The first fish to bite was that old ass nigga. Sam. He was a former state prison guard that retired two years before. He was living off his pension and retirement benefits. He was married, so I kept it simple with him. I told him that for $200, we can get a room and he can fuck and suck me all he wanted for two hours. Sammy got us a room at a Motel 8 near the bus station. I met him there, he handed me my cash, and then we got to it. He had two hours with me, but he only lasted an hour. First of all, he wasn't working with much. Five inches of mostly limp, old penis. I was sucking his dick for less than five minutes when he grabbed my hair in both fists, started "trying" to ram in my throat; nearly screaming that he was cumming. I didn't let him bust in my mouth. I stroked his nut onto my neck & titties. I let him lay on the bed and catch his breath while I cleaned his semen off me, before grabbing a condom out of my purse.

I climbed up on the bed with him. Stroking his dick and massaging his balls until he was hard again. I then rolled the lifestyle condom onto his dick, straddled him, guided his latex covered penis into my wet pussy, and started riding his old ass. Sam looked like he was gonna have a stroke on me as I rode him towards paradise. I took him as deep as his five-inch dick could go, put his hands on my titties, made him look into my eyes, and snake rolled my pelvis with my vaginal muscle's lobster clawing his shaft. Sam thought he was fucking me, but I in reality; I was fucking him. I had him positioned so that I ride him and focus stimulation on my G-spot. Only my sugar daddy was a TDN. A Tender Dicked Nigga. I rode him slow and deep for a while, then I switched up and started bouncing harder and faster. Sam gripped my waist with his head back, making a lot of noise with his eyes shut. I bit into my bottom lip as I used my pussy to vaporize his old soul. I was super wet too. Sam grabbed my ass cheeks as I bounced. He moaned as he came into the condom, but I kept going until I had my orgasm too. Which nearly killed the old motherfucker.

As I smoked a cigarette in my bra and panties, I asked Sam was he ready to go again? We had a little over an hour left before he had to go home. He was laid out the bed, looking sleepy and satisfied as he smiled while telling me nah. He was good. Then added that he would go another round with me, but he wasn't young no more. Ease up on an old man. We both laughed as I replied, cool. I told him to call me when he wanted to have some fun again as I gathered my stuff, made my way into the bathroom, and cleaned up. I emerged twenty-minutes later. Freshly showered and dressed. Because I kind of liked Sam, before I left, I kissed him on the forehead and whispered, *"Till next time, boo."* As I left the motel room. My cab was waiting for me near the office. As the driver pulled off, I lit a cigarette before taking out my phone and checking a message. One of the hustlers I met, a twenty-six-year-old dope boy, agreed to my terms. $100 to suck his dick until he bust. Not a problem. That's what he wanted, that's what he's going to get. I texted him back. Requesting his location before lowering my phone and taking a pull on my cigarette while watching night time Columbus whiz by.

****

That's how I made my money. Day after day. Week in and week out. For three months straight. I built myself a black book of sugar daddies & hustling tricks. Dealing with the older niggas was pretty much an easy and simple affair. They just wanted some young pussy. They paid for head and sex from a younger woman and that was that. I met up with them, collected my money, I made them feel good, and then we went our separate ways. The older dudes understood what it was. A no-strings attached cash for sex transaction. A lot of the younger hustling niggas understood that too. For those that did, it was a little more than just the sex. Any chick can give a nigga some pussy and he happy, but when you look deeper into most men; it's all about their ego. The hustlers in my black book had no problem paying for my time because they loved fucking me, as much as they loved looking at a sexy woman such as me. Every man I lied with complimented me. From my hair, to my eyes, face, lips, skin tone, my titties, curves, butt, and every other body part they enjoyed looking at, touching, and tasting.

More than half of the men I saw kept shit simple and sweet. I got paid and occasionally had an orgasm while satisfying their loins & egos. Then, there were my headaches. The greedy motherfuckers. Those few niggas that weren't satisfied. I had to stop seeing one of my sugar daddies and three of my hustlers. All four of them started going against the grain. They became clingy, needy, pushy, and clearly thought that I was their fuckin' girlfriend. All of them would send me WYD texts, frequently call me bae or boo, call me in the middle of the night when I was asleep, and one pressed up on me like we were married when I was at a bar one night. I was in mid-conversation with this cute ass nigga when one of my tricks interrupted us. He was acting like I was his wife

46

and he caught me out on a date with another man. I checked his ass right then and there. With no trace of mercy or restraint.

I cussed his five-foot six, moderately cute ass straight the fuck out! Embarrassing him in front of the bar as I told him all about himself and the fact that he was insecure and jealous of the chick that he was paying to fuck on the side; when he had a whole fiancée at home! I don't know if it was my acid laced words or people's laughter that made my ex-trick bounce like he did; nor did I care. Business had its ups and downs. The niggas that understood the game made shit easy for me. All of them were paying me for one form of sexual pleasure or the other. Most wanted to fuck, a few had a fetish for eating pussy *(which was fine by me)*, and every single one of them wanted their dicks sucked. For some, that's all they wanted. Or, only had time for. The dudes that got sprung on me were the ones that had a woman at home, or desperately wanted one.

As the months went by, while stacking my money, I started studying men more closely. The names in my black book that kept it strictly to business were always the older niggas. They knew from the door exactly what it was. They were coughing up their money to a beautiful younger woman for the satisfaction of a sexual release. We got along, conversation was always easy, and they didn't press me for more than what we had. None of them tried to take me out on a real date, text me like we were in love, randomly call me, or try to coerce me into a relationship. Like most of the younger dudes did. The thirty-four and under motherfuckers in my book were my headaches. One out of three either attempted to pressure me into being with them, acted like we were married, tried to boo love & snuggle with me, or reveal that they were possessive ass psychopaths. I developed a radar for men with issues and began to reject them from being added to my list of tricks. After five months of stacking cash, I wanted to put in one more month and then leave Columbus.

Las Vegas was my goal destination. I accepted the fact that I was a call girl and began researching the trade. There were seven cities in America where a chick can make major money and live a life of total luxury as a call girl. New York City, Washington D.C., Atlanta, Miami, Chicago, Los Angeles, and Vegas. Sin City was the #1 location to make real money in the cash for sex game. That was my ambition. Until one of my tricks forced me to alter my schedule. His name was Marcel Morris and he was one fine motherfucker. Six-two, built like a boxer, twenty-nine-years old, cute as fuck, brown skinned, a serious player in the Columbus drug game. OMG he was packing a cannon between his legs. Marcel was the only nigga I slept with that satisfied me, just as much as I satisfied him. Cell got the premium package with me. He wasn't shy about spending money either. For $1000, he had me for an entire night.

From the time we checked into a hotel in the evening, until early the next morning; I gave Marcel anything he wanted. My mouth, pussy, even some anal action. Sex with him was off the chain!! That nigga made me cum over and over, harder and harder. His tongue was fire and his stroke was elite! I even liked hanging out with him after and in between our sex sessions. He was funny, charming, a great conversationalist, fun to be around, and I actually liked spending the night with him. That is until he had to go and fuck it all up. By dropping hints that he wanted to be with me. He made subtle suggestions that he could take care of me, that we looked good together, and that he was developing feelings for me. Once he started in with that kind of dialogue; I had to cut him off. I texted Marcel after I caught on to him trying to wife me up. To inform him that it's been fun knowing him and I wished him well; but I was no longer interested in seeing him anymore. Goodbye. I deleted his number, blocked him from contacting me, and that was that.

Or so I thought it was. I ran into Marcel a week later. At a club. I was at the bar enjoying a drink and chillin'. I spoke to a couple of niggas, a few gave me their number, but on that night, I wasn't looking to add any more clients to my list. Occasionally, I took some time to myself. Most of week was spent catering to men's sexual needs. At least two days a week was my time. On this particular Saturday night, I was blowing off some steam. It was a good day for me. I got in a two hour work out at the gym, did some shopping, took my new ride to the car wash, enjoyed a delicious solo lunch at a Bistro, kept my mani-pedi appointment, and then smoked some bomb ass weed before ordering some Chinese. I was going to stay in, but I decided fuck it. I might as well hit a club or two.

Big mistake. I wish I had kept my ass home that night. I was in a club for about an hour and a half and was sitting at a table with a sexy as fuck light skinned nigga; enjoying a drink and some nice conversation. Dude was actually making me blush and smile a little. Just as I was thinking about taking ol' boy to a hotel for the night and riding his handsome as face, just for my own pleasure; Marcel suddenly appeared. He went in on me like I was his wife; that just caught cheating on him. He aggressively demanded to know why the fuck I blocked him and he hasn't heard from me?! I narrowed my eyes at his crazy, pussy whipped ass. I sat my martini on the table, stood up, and got right in his face. With my stiletto's on, I was damn near eye level with him. I wasn't his woman, nor was I scared of anyone. Man or woman. So right there in the middle of the club, I attempted to check this out-of-pocket motherfucker. I say attempt, because Marcel's obsessed, maniac ass did something I didn't see coming.

In the middle of my profanity laced verbal onslaught, he put his hands on me. I forgot that he used to box. In the blink of an eye, he caught me mid-rant with a lightning quick two-piece combination. I saw two bright, blue & white camera flashes before I felt myself hit the floor. There was a loud, echoing whine in my ears, I could hear myself breathing, and though I wasn't knocked out and could see; my vision was hazy and doubled. I tasted warm-coppery blood in my mouth and my face was numb. My hand felt heavy as I brought it up to cheek and I just lied there. I saw flashing spots, movement, and I heard the hollow sound of music and yelling. It felt like forever until I regained my senses at the same time a face came into view. A dark brown skinned brother with a bald head and a heavy beard. It took me a moment to recognize him. He was one of the bouncers. His voice sounded far away and was echoing as he advised me to lie still. Don't try to get up. That there was an ambulance on the way.

****

I was taken to the emergency room, triaged, given an ice pack, a nurse checked my eyes with a tiny flashlight, and then I was wheeled up to the radiology floor. For an X-Ray. Once they were done, one of the aides transported me back to my ER room to wait for the results of the scan. I swallowed an 800-milligram Ibuprofen for my pounding headache and the pain to my right eye and left cheek. Both were swollen and hurt like a bitch. As I sat there, barely able to see on the right, tears streamed down my puffed-out cheek from my left eye. The police had already come and gone. Marcel was restrained by security and turned over to the cops once they arrived at the club. The detective that interviewed me told me that a couple of witnesses gave a statement that Marcel has struck me as we were arguing. When he asked me was that true, I said yes. He then asked me how he and I knew each other? I replied that we dated for a while but had recently broken up. The detective wrote down my answers, then asked one final question.

Did I want to press charges? Yes, I immediately replied. He wrote a few more things down, then pulled out a document from his leather binder. He explained to me that it was an official victims' statement. All I had to do was sign and date it on the required lines, he'll type up my account of the assault for the report, then submit it to the prosecutors' office. An ADA will contact me within twenty-four hours. For the time being though, Marcel will be processed and charged with assault and battery in the first degree. The detective gave me one of his cards, apologized for what my "ex" did to me, and hoped that I quickly recovered. I had just about fallen asleep when my X-Ray results came back. Nothing was broken and there was no major damage, but the swelling to my eye and cheek were serious. The ER doctor wrote ordered two prescriptions. A pain killer and an anti-inflammatory. She advised me to ice my cheek and a warm compress on my eye to help with the swelling. I was then discharged, got dressed, and caught a cab from the hospital back to the club. To pick up my car.

I drove back to my apartment and went straight to the bathroom. For a long time, I stared at myself in the mirror. Marcel really fucked my face up. My eye was just about swollen shut and my black-purple bruised cheek was all puffed out. My nose felt broken, my front teeth hurt, there was blood crusting in my nostrils, and I still tasted it in my mouth. As I stared at my reflection, my pounding-aching brain was a toxic mix of anger and sadness. I studied Marcel's handiwork and blamed both of us. Him for being such a pussy whipped, emotionally weak, possessive, and egotistical fuck boy. Me for still craving some form of love, acceptance, security, and for allowing him to make me feel vulnerable. Marcel was a nigga that lived in a fantasy world. H believed that he could make a pretty call girl his woman and I violated my rule. I let a motherfucker get too close to me. I broke my rule and he broke my face. I sighed as I exited my bathroom. Lesson learned.

For the next eight days, I lived inside my apartment. I mostly crashed on my couch, dressed in sweats and a t-shirt, watching TV and movies. That's also where I slept, ate, smoked, and relaxed. Every time I left my place, I wore a hoody or sunglasses and I didn't stay out very long. I went to whatever store I needed to visit and I took my ass back home. I didn't really care what anyone would think of my black eye and bruised cheek, but I just didn't want motherfuckers staring at me. Or, have women in my face to extend their solidarity and support as if I was domestic violence victim. I also deactivated my work phone. I knew my clients were all broken up that they couldn't get their dicks wet with me anymore; but oh well. I was done with Columbus. Over the eight days I was in isolation, even though I was lying on the couch staring at my TV screen, or lying on my back smoking a blunt; I was game planning. It was time to take my shit to the next level.

I spent that week debating on which city I wanted to relocate to. I had a close to $60,000 in cash and another $5,500 in my bank account. Over the six months I tricked with niggas, on average, I banked $1,200 a week. I always saved far more than I spent, so I did more stacking than spending. My goal was to hit 40 to 50k before I got the fuck out of Ohio. I figured that with a minimum of $50,000 I could set up wherever I went and get back on the grind. The situation with Marcel forced me to change my time table. I wanted to get the Hell out of Columbus, step my game up, and focus on changing the way I did business. My initial thought was to head to NYC. I always wanted to do it big in the Big Apple, but I hate the cold and I heard that New York winters can be brutal. That went for Philly and D.C. as well. Baltimore was no go, I pondered on Atlanta, but after researching the rampant STD rate amongst the men: I struck ATL off my list. I considered Miami, but those damn Hurricanes made me scratch Florida too. That left Chicago, Vegas, and LA.

I went back and forth with myself for days before I finally made my decision. Los Angeles, but after I padded my bank in Nevada. I spent almost an entire day studying and reading up on the action in Las Vegas. Prostituting, the call girl game, and escorting was serious in Sin City. I watched a couple of YouTube videos of chicks that made their money out there. I was hooked. Bitches, not even top shelf chicks, were banking major cash out there and I wanted in! Thus, I ignored the calls from the prosecutor handling Marcel's case, packed what I was taking with me, loaded up my car, stopped at a gas station to fill my tank and buy a load of junk food, plugged Las Vegas, Nevada into my GPS, said goodbye to Ohio. It was me, my cigarettes, music, 2,000 miles, and thirty-hours of driving towards my ambitions. All I had in this world was money, freedom to do what I want, and my damn self.

I needed nothing, from anyone, for anything.

CHAPTER FIVE

"Money is a number and numbers never end.
If it takes money for you to be happy,
Your search for happiness will never end."

-Bob Marley

My arrival in Las Vegas was like some shit out of a damn movie. It took me close to three days to make that long ass drive from Ohio to Nevada. I stopped to rest every six hours after driving for almost eighteen hours straight. I checked into a motel twice, refilled my gas tank four times, and pulled off the highway to eat whenever my stomach started to rumble. Other than that, I smoked cigarettes, sipped bottle water, and put off stopping for food by munching on chips and whatnot. I was four hours from Vegas and it was getting dark when I took the exit off the interstate and decided to check into a Travel-lodge motel a few miles from the highway. I got a ground room floor, took a shower, and went right to bed. I had a headache and my eyes hurt. It was just after 7:30 pm when I closed my eyes. Six hours later, the alarm on my phone went off and I was up. I stopped at an all-night diner, had myself a double cheese burger with onion rings and a milkshake, then it was back onto the Nevada interstate.

Five hours later, just as the sky was turning to day and all pretty with multiple-colored clouds and the rising sun; I saw Vegas in the distance. It was early morning, so nothing was really happening on the strip. Still, I cruised around; marveling at everything. The hotels and casinos, all the tourist attractions, and things that I've only seen on TV. I found myself rolling through the hood. I spotted prostitutes and pimps, bums, wino's, and drug dealers of all races. I pulled into a McDonald's drive-thru, got myself a coffee and sausage McMuffin, then parked in the lot. To look up the motels in the city. I found the one that best fit what I needed and followed the GPS to my destination. The Nevada Inn. The kind of motel that had rooms that were more like small apartments. I rented a second level corner unit for three months up front. The middle-aged white owner was happy as fuck with me moving in. At $175 a week, he looked like a little kid on Christmas morning when I put $2100 in his hand.

My new place was ok for the time being. It was by no mean large or luxurious, but there was adequate space to accommodate me. It was also clean, the bed was a queen size, the bathroom was decent, the kitchen-dining room area was alright, and there was a 32-inch flat screen TV. I moved my shit in, took a long hot shower, ordered some Mexican food, smoked half a blunt, ate, and then with the TV on, door locked, and blinds pulled down; I went to sleep. I was exhausted, my head and neck were killing me, and all I wanted was a full night of uninterrupted rest. I woke up nine and a half hours later. It was starting to get dark when I opened my eyes. I lied there for a while, staring at the ceiling and ignoring the sound of the low-volume television as I prepared my mind for my quest. Vegas was a gold mine city in the southwest to get paid. I had all the assets necessary to get rich and find happiness & luxury in this life.

I was young and pretty in the face with a sexy body. I took great care of myself, I knew how to dress, my sexual forte was top-shelf, and I knew how to finesse motherfuckers with deep pockets and sensitive dicks. I grinned as I rose up from the bed to get ready for my first night in Vegas. It was time for step one. Get a lay of the land. Feel out the scene. Catch the vibe of Sin City and then put my game plan into action. An hour after I woke up, I exited my motel room. Conservatively dressed but still sexy. I had on a form fitting black blouse. Opened three buttons to expose my cleavage, skin tight dark blue jeans, and a pair of black leather ankle high stiletto boots. My hair was in a simple long-straight style, I put on a little make up, glossed my lips, dashed on some perfume, and decided to rock my diamond stud earrings. On my way to my car, I got hit on by one of the motel residents. A tall and stocky-pudgy brown skinned nigga with a do-rag, tank top and basketball shorts on. He was at least forty. Sitting on a fold out chair in front of his room.

Mr. Ex-con with the not so well-groomed beard, dingy socks, and worn out Nike slides tried to capture my attention as I walked by. I ghosted him as I passed by his room. His voice was friendly and inviting when he was attempting to get me to stop and talk to him, but when I didn't bother to even acknowledge his existence; his tone immediately changed. To subtle anger, passively hostile, and disrespectful as he shot, *"Fuck you too, you stuck up bitch!"* I smirked to myself as I walked through the gate, making a mental note to acquire myself some protection. My instincts were telling me that he was probably going to take a shot at. He had that aggressive with women vibe to him. Thus, I was going buy myself three things that I will keep in my purse. A knife, pepper spray, and one of those spring out police batons. I was a felon, so buying a gun was off the table. Still. After getting my face busted in by Marcel, I was done playing games with men. The next motherfucker that makes me fear for my safety or I even think he's going to put his fuckin' hands on me; they'll be the ones in the damn emergency room!

****

My stomach was empty, as was my gas tank. I stopped to fill both of them. I found a four-star Chinese buffet and went into get my grub on. Once I was done eating, I cruised around Vegas for a while. Checking out the ebb and flow on the strip, peeped out the action in front of the hotels & casinos, then I rolled past several strip clubs. After finding a safe place to park my car, I got out and strolled on foot. It wasn't even the weekend and the Vegas nightlife was live and jumping. Expensive cars and SUV's were cruising up and down the strip, there were lights everywhere, and there were mad people out and about. Most of them looked like normal everyday residents, but I spotted the odd balls. Tourists, hustlers, dope heads, bums, hookers, and weirdos. Twice, I got hit on by a pimp. One was black and thought it was still the 1970's. He had a short afro, an open powder blue silk shirt, tight white pants, leather boots, and a clean-shaven face. I was passing by a bar and he was standing in front of it with his ho's.

On a scale of one-to-ten, his bitches were a three at best. Both of them were youngish looking white girls in skanky ho wear. They looked strung out too. I didn't stop walking as their pimp called out to me. In a futile attempt to get me to stop and talk to him. I glanced at him as he spoke with a cigar clenched between his gold ringed fingers. I never slowed down or looked back at him, ignoring his, *"Hey there baby, can I talk to ya for a minute?...Come on, sweet thang, let me hollah at ya real quick."* I shook my head and kept on walking. That pathetic ass pimp daddy didn't have a chance in Hell with me. One, I may be young; but I'm not dumb. Nor am I weak. Two? What the fuck I look like walking the ho stroll? Flagging motherfuckers down to suck and fuck in their vehicle, or in some seedy motel to line a niggas pockets while getting slapped around and beat on??! Strung out on drugs and shit. Nah. Not me. My pussy has a market value on it, but I was in charge. I decided the price, who I fucked, and when I fucked them. Not some nigga in an imitation silk shirt with a pinky ring.

It was a little after 9:00 pm and I was chilling in the bar & lounge of the MGM grand hotel. The place was beyond nice and better than any spot I ever been to. There were quite a few people scattered around and the music was smooth. I sat by myself. Away from everyone. Watching and taking everything in. I spotted couples on dates, chicks vacationing with their home girls, people having a quiet drink after work, and the ladies of the night. I sipped a vodka & cranberry while studying the working girls. There was a mixture of call girls and escorts doing their thing around the bar. It took me a minute, but I noted the difference. The call girls strolled into the lounge, linked up with their client, they hung out for a few minutes, then they left together. Presumably heading for their tricks room to get down to business.

The escorts met up with their dates, but they didn't quickly depart with them. Those beautiful and well-dressed women met the men paying for their time at the bar or a table, sat down, they ordered a drink, and conversation commenced. From my vantage point, it looked like they were on an actual date. I watched those women smile, laugh, and subtly flirt with the men they were meeting. A few even left the lounge arm-in-arm with their dates; heading for the restaurant across the way. During my research on escorts, these women did have sex with their clients, but they weren't like call girls and prostitutes.

Escorts were well trained, intimate companions. They really did go on dates with the men paying them for their time. They were professional girlfriend-lovers. They had meaningful conversations with their clients, were very intelligent, classy, and could masterfully cater to a man's every desire. The best escorts were developed in what they called charm schools. Private and secret academy-like institutions where veteran escorts trained the rookies. That sounded nice and all, but I didn't have time for all that.

I was going to learn as I worked. Watch, study, and emulate as I made my money. Starting tonight. I cruised the casino's and bars for a few hours until I found my first potential pony. I engaged in conversation with various dudes that approached me; but rejected them all. Until I came across a reasonably cute thirty-one-year-old white guy named Josh. I was sitting at the bar at the Bellagio. Nursing another vodka & cranberry. As I was lighting a cigarette, I pretended that I didn't know that the sharply bearded white boy with the white shirt & loose tie hasn't been checking me out. I finally looked his way, flashed him a sweet & seductive smile, slowly exhaled, and then indicated with my head for him to come on over. He smiled almost shyly, grabbed his glass of what looked like whiskey, and strolled over to where I was sitting. I turned on my stool with a bright smile. He extended his hand, I took it, and we introduced ourselves as we shook. Josh took the stool next to me and we started talking.

He bought a round of drinks and I smoked another cigarette as we got to know each other a little. He told me that he was single, lived alone, had no kids, and worked as a mechanical engineer for a development company. Josh believed my name was Nia, I was from Detroit, just turned twenty-two-years old, I also had no kids, and I moved to Vegas to make some money before heading to LA to become a model. Conversation with Josh was cool and relaxed, but after making small talk for about fifteen-minutes or so; I decided to be direct. I knew within two minutes that he wanted to fuck; but I strung him along just to make sure. I leaned in close, and softly playing with his fingers, I put it out there. I whispered that for $500, I was his to enjoy for two hours. I didn't have to look at his crotch to see his dick get hard. It was evident in his pretty green eyes. He nodded his head, agreeing to my offer. That's when I motioned for him to come close and I whispered in his ear. I then pulled back, stubbed my cigarette out, and went back to my drink as he exited the bar to hit an AT. Then get himself a room for the night.

Less than half an hour later, I was on the bed of a room on the sixth floor of the Bellagio. Moaning with my eyes closed and head turned to the side as Josh ate my pussy. I kept one hand on the back of his head as sucked and licked on my clit. Normally I didn't get too turned on when handling business; but white boy was making me feel good. It had been a while since I got some and though I was making $500 for two hours of work; when he requested to eat me out, I didn't hesitate to let him do his thing. Josh had his whole face buried in my pussy. Going hard and fast with his mouth. He even tongue fucked me. By the time he made me cum, I was soaking the sheet and his face. He then put on the condom I gave him, I opened my legs, watched him guide his slightly thick, seven, seven and a half inch, pale pink-reddish dick into me. I held onto his hips as he started stroking away.

No, he wasn't hitting deep, but his dick felt good though. Josh was making more noise than I was, but I encouraged him. I moaned a little for him, bit my lip, told him how good he felt, I moved my hips to meet his strokes, and I licked my lips. The more he stroked, the wetter I got. Thus, the more I was turning him on. So much in fact, that he kept trying to kiss me as if we lovers. I let him kiss my lips, but I refused to let him put his tongue in my mouth. Every time he tried, I moved away. Turned my head to the side and keep meeting his thrusts with my hips. Kissing was act of intimacy. An act of passion. Love. This was none of that. This was a man paying a woman to fuck her. This was strictly sex. Josh stopped trying to kiss me. He licked & sucked on my neck instead. Then my titties. We went from missionary, to doggy style, then I got on top and rode his dick for a while. Regular, then reverse cowgirl. We finished round one on the dresser. He had my legs up and tried to fuck my brains out until he was busting off inside the condom. Loud, animated, and covered in sweat.

Round two was twenty minutes after round one. This time I gave Josh head, he ate me out again from the back, and then he lasted for about ten loud moaning minutes until he came again and ran out of gas. We smoked a cigarette and he stretched out on the bed as I went into the bathroom to take a quick shower and get ready to leave. When I came out, there was no bullshit from Josh. I took his number and told him that I will call him when I set up my new phone. We then hugged and I left. $500 richer. On my way back to the motel, I stopped for food and picked up a bottle of Henny. Mr. Do-rag wasn't outside his room when I arrived, but I did get hit on by a trio of young looking thugs. Two were black and there was a lone white boy that thought he was black. Just like my neighbor that called me a stuck-up bitch for not responding to him; I ghosted the three amigos as I walked past them. Once in my room, I locked the door, made sure my blinds were fully closed, turned my TV on, and my night was done.

****

Nine weeks went by. Josh was my first client in Vegas. After our first date, he became a black book regular. I met up with him three more times before I gained my second client. A handsome nightlife promoter by the name of James Raymond Miller. The chocolate brown skinned, sharp suit wearing, former middleweight boxer turned businessman became my second regular after we met at one of his clubs. He thought I was just another young black chick with a pretty face and fat ass. Over a drink in the VIP section of his spot, I showed him that I wasn't just another thot he was gonna slide dick up in because he was smooth and well known. James was the arrogant type, so he agreed to pay to play, but he had to make a point. He hit me off with a thousand dollars and we went back to his condo a few miles off the strip. Once there, he went all

57

in on me. That muscle-bound motherfucker licked, fucked, and sucked my ass silly. His fetish was a woman's booty. He mostly fucked me from the back, grabbing & slapping my ass, he made me ride him reverse cowgirl, and his hands rarely left my ass cheeks. When it came to head, he liked it wet, deep, fast, and sloppy.

Within nine weeks, I have six names in my black book. Four were big spenders and two were average spending clients. The high rollers routinely dropped anywhere from $500-$1000 per date. My other two spent between $200-$400 with me. Either way, I was banking dough. Serious dough. I split my savings between my bank account, two safety deposit boxes, and a mobile safe in my room. I learned my lesson from the Raheem situation. Never keep all my money in one spot. Once I had a steady stream of income, I settled back into a routine. My days started off in the gym, I kept my appointments with the hair & nail salons, I joined a boxing club, and when I wasn't working out or taking care of my body; I cruised around Vegas. I made and lost money in the casinos, got to know the bartenders and bouncers, I started building business relationships with exotic dancers, and I actually made a real friend. With another young chick that was in Sin City to stack her money.

Her name was Brandi Watts. She went by Karina with her clients though. Like me, she hailed from the Midwest. Chicago to be exact. Brandi and I met at a low-key lounge just off the strip. It was a quiet, laid back spot that catered to the mellow crowd. Older people. I liked it there because I could drink and smoke in peace while listening to live Jazz, spoken word artists, and able to decompress. On the night Brandi and I came together, she was sitting at a table close to mine, doing the same thing I was doing. Chilling by herself with a drink. Content to sit back and relax. Even in the dim atmosphere of the lounge, I noted that she was very pretty. Light skinned, with shoulder length brown hair, a big chest, and I was digging her dress style. Similar to my own. Conservative, with a flair of sexual temptation. I was catching a cool vibe from her, so I decided to bend my rule. On making friends. I waved a server over to my table, ordered another martini for myself, then I paid for whatever Brandi was drinking and told the cute server to let her know that it was from me.

A short while later, Brandi and I introduced ourselves to one another. After she thanked me for another Absolut & lemon on ice. I extended an offer for her to sit with me and she accepted. We started talking and the flow of conversation between us was perfect. After exchanging basic information and a few laughs, feeling each other out, we shared the same reality. The reason both of us were in Vegas. She was twenty-one, I was nineteen, and we were two young black women chasing the bag. When Brandi suggested that we leave, I agreed. We departed the lounge and decided to go get something to eat. I followed her car across the city to a black owned restaurant and we went in to enjoy some soul food and conversation. Over a late-night dinner, we shared our stories. I told mine first, then she did the same. Brandi was from the south side of Chicago and the second oldest of five. She once had three brothers and a sister. Until her big sister, the oldest of all five of them was killed during a gang shooting on their block. One of her brothers was in prison for drug trafficking, another was in college on a basketball scholarship, and the other decided to get the fuck out of Chicago. By joining the army.

Brandi's parents were the typical sad ass chapter in the story of Black America. Her dad was full-on dead beat. She and her older sister shared the same father, but he was never such. Just another nigga that put his dick in a woman with no desire to raise his kids. He was in and out of jail, on and off drugs, and revolving alcoholic, a womanizer, and a pathetic excuse for a criminal. Brandi told me that her dad was a consistent liar, excuse maker, and promise breaker. Her mom raised her, but she was no better. Even after having five kids, it was all about her. She was a bar hopping, party hard type of female that was more concerned about looking good, taking care of herself, chasing good for nothing niggas, and projecting her anger and frustration on children. Brandi looked like she was about to cry, but she didn't. She just kept talking about her life and I listened to her. The only person she loved and counted on was her big sister. Then nine years before, she was killed right in front of her. Two gangs opened fire on each other during a block party and her sister was shot.

Dying in her little sisters' arms as she screamed for help. Things only got worse for Brandi a year later. When she was repeatedly raped by one of her mother's boyfriends. A grown man that threatened a young girl with violence if she didn't "make him feel good". For nearly six months, she was repeatedly molested by him, until she finally told someone. One of the women in the neighborhood. Her rapist was arrested, but Brandi's mom blamed her daughter. Sending her to live with her aunt in Joliet, Illinois. Where she first became a wild teenager, then a chick that fucked with thugs and hustlers, and when her aunt and her man were arrested for selling dope; Child services tried to place her in foster care. Brandi had other plans though. She ran away. Doing what she had to do to survive. Using sex to get by until she relocated to Vegas to chase the American dream. Money, luxury, and freedom. It was while telling me her story that I saw something special in Brandi. I knew I wasn't the only chick out here that been through that horrible shit or lived how I did; but in her, I saw something. Something that drew me to her.

I saw that for the first time in a long time I wasn't alone. I felt connected to Brandi. Our life stories were similar, our vibe was similar, and we were in the same place, doing the same thing, for the same reason. We talked through dinner and outside standing next to our cars as we smoked. I truly sensed the beginning of a real friendship, so being that we both were avid exercisers, I invited her to meet me at 24-hour Fitness in the morning. Brandi immediately agreed, we exchanged numbers, hugged, then went our separate ways. In the morning, at 9:30 am, I watched her pull up in her platinum-colored Mazda 6 and park next to my champagne colored Buick Regal Sportback. Both of our rides were clean, sleek, and despite being pre-owned; looked new. I climbed out my vehicle with in a white Nike Jogging suit with my gym bag. Brandi was dressed in a black Reebok sports top and yoga pants, book bag slung over one shoulder. Both of us had our hair back in pony tails and being thoughtful, I handed her a large plastic cup of probiotic berry infused fruit juice with ice as we headed inside to get our workout on.

We were in 24-Hour fitness for two and a half hours. Though we stayed together, Brandi and I went about our own workout routine. We stretched together, helped each other loosen up, then made our way to the universal cable machines. I worked on my shoulders and arms for a while, then moved to my legs. I did squats with dumbbells, leg lifts, then lunges. Brandi focused on his arms and legs, then we did crunches and knee lifts while hanging from the pull-up bar. After a short break, while I jogged a few miles on the treadmill, my new friend was short distance away on a stationary bike. She had earbuds wired to her phone while I jogged with wireless buds connected to my I-POD. We took a water and chill break, then made our way to the heavy bag. I had an extra pair of gloves, so we took turns holding the bag for each other and punching it for three minutes at time. Brandi and I worked up a good sweat working out, then we went down stairs to the sauna room. Wearing only towels, we sat close to each other and talked. Surrounded by steam, we discussed how we individually conducted business.

Our conversation continued after we showered, got dressed, and linked up in the parking lot. We smoked as we stood with our backs to our cars. Discussing a possible partnership. I liked the idea, but I let

Brandi know something upfront. I didn't really trust or believe in people. I had no reason to. She nodded her head and replied that she felt the same way. We held eyes for a moment, then I broke the silence by keeping it real with her. I stated that I was going to take a chance with her, if she was willing to take a chance with me. Yes, I felt the start of a beautiful friendship, but when it comes to my money and my safety. I can't afford to have any doubts in her. Brandi acknowledged my position and told me that she was on the same page. If we were going to do this, then trust is the one thing that is non-negotiable. She then looked me in my eyes and told me that I could trust her, she was going to take a risk and trust me, and she believed that we met for a reason. A real friend is a rarity in this world. She felt that our meeting one another was not an accident or coincidence. I smirked as I agreed with her, then suggested that we go somewhere for lunch. I was hungry as Hell.

Over a delicious meal at a steakhouse, Brandi and I discussed the outline of our partnership. Being that we conducted business in similar fashion, it was easy to develop a format of how we could work together. Since she's been in Vegas longer than me, I let her take the lead. She told me the in's and outs of the city, what casino's and clubs were the best to scout new clients, and we kept it simple. We both had our black book of clients and agreed to never share them. Or, poach them. Those were our guaranteed money makers on the solo end. Brandi and I were on the same page when it came to working in tandem. Together. She shared her ideas on how we'll work as a team and I added in my thoughts. We formed a solid game plan and I couldn't wait to see how it played out. Brandi and I touched wine glasses together, toasting to our new friendship and partners in crime. I envisioned us making money together, but I saw something else too.

The beginning of a real and lasting bond.

CHAPTER SIX

"The longer you dance with the Devil,
the longer you remain in Hell."

Four months went by and I felt on top of the world. Brandi was far more than my friend by this point. She was my friend, partner, and my lover. Two months after meeting each other, we move in together. Before her, I never thought about another female in an intimate / sexual way. Even though it didn't happen right away, when it did, I liked it. Loved it. For weeks after met, it was mostly business between us. We met up to work out together, shop, get our hair & nails done, and we went out to eat. Other than that, we did our thing as we were before coming together. She met with her clients for dates and I met with mine. Brandi and I did talk and text more and more as time went by. Forty-nine days after meeting, she hit me up as I was chilling at my spot. It was a Sunday evening, so it was my day off. My work phone was powered down and fully charged. My second phone was on the charger when Brandi called me. I was smoking a joint filled with some bomb Kush that I got from a white girl that worked as a server in the bar at the Bellagio.

Between a hot shower, dildo session as I air dried, weed, and the white wine I was sipping as I watched Bad Girls Club; I was nice. Relaxed and just chillin'. Brandi called to ask me if I was ready for our first double date? I grinned as I replied, *"Hell yeah!"* She informed me that she had the details, but didn't want to share them over the phone. I agreed and she asked me to meet her at a bar called Sundown. Once I had the address, I told her that I'll meet her there in twenty. Twenty-five minutes later, B and I had some privacy in a booth in the back of the bar. She arrived first, so when I showed up, there was a drink waiting for me. My favorite Vodka and cranberry with crushed ice. We immediately got down to business. She told me that our tandem date was with two high rollers. She showed me their picture on her phone. The two brothers in the pic were sexy as fuck! One was a light skinned, delicious looking pretty boy. His homie was my flavor. Dark chocolate sexiness.

Devin Stevens and Lamar Dayne were best friends and business partners in Los Angeles. Their friendship went all the way back to their childhood. Brandi gave me the goods on them. Devin, the gorgeous redbone, was once an NBA prospect that was big time at UCLA; Lamar was an NFL bound wide receiver for the same university. Unfortunately, Devin blew out his knee and Lamar didn't make the cut for the Denver Broncos as an undrafted rookie. The two of them returned to Inglewood and got into the drug game, but then turned their blood money into something of worth. They opened up legit businesses and used the profits to climb the ladder of success. One of their highest profiting endeavors was a gentleman's club in downtown LA. A club that only featured the sexiest women as dancers and catered almost exclusively to VIP's. Devin and Lamar were friends with celebrities in the music business, the movie industry, and the professional sports world.

Brandi met Devin on Instagram. He liked a bunch of her pictures and then DM'd her. The two of them talked and she let on to the fact that she was an independent operator. Her code name for professional companion. Devin was obviously game, because he didn't hesitate to open negotiations with her. Brandi upped the ante by informing him that she had a partner for his homie. Being that the two of them were going to be in Vegas and they already planned to see each other while he was in town. I was all for the date with my friend and she grinned as she told me that it was time for me to do my part. Lamar liked the picture she sent to Devin to show him and was waiting for me to contact him. I did just that. I took out my phone, Brandi gave me his Instagram screen name, I requested him, and less than ten minutes later, he accepted me and hit my DM. B was on the phone as Lamar and I felt each other out, settled on how much a date with me will cost him, and that was that. Not only was I going to hook up with a sexy and smooth rich nigga; I was making $4,000 for one date.

Three days later, Brandi and I arrived at the Mandalay Bay hotel dressed and pressed to kill. We went all out. Most of the day was spent preparing for this night. We hit the gym, the salon, got our legs waxed, and we decided to go with a blend of sexy and classy with our outfits. Brandi had on a matte black V-neck asymmetrical mini dress and three-inch stilettos. I went with a shimmering black, off the shoulders, long-sleeved bodycon mini dress. My heels were three-inch as well, but I was rocking Christian Louboutin red bottoms. B had on Gucci. Our hair and nails were on point, we smelled good, my pussy was shaven smooth, both of us were shining in jewels and carrying leather clutch purses. Brandi gave her name to the concierge at the front desk and he cleared us to access the VIP level elevator. He passed her an elevator keycard and off we went. We took the reserved elevator up to the 15th floor and our dates were waiting for us. Here we go, I thought to myself. Smiling as we approached Devin and Lamar.

Before the real fun began, Brandi and I were catered to. Devin & Lamar, both of whom looked good as fuck in their GQ attire, were on some real gentlemen shit. They greeted us with chivalry, shaking and kissing the back of our hands, and then escorting us to the patio with a beautiful view of Vegas. They offered us a seat at a round glass table. There was a bottle of champagne in a silver bucket and four crystal glasses. Lamar sat down beside me as Devin filled our glasses with Veuve Clicquot La Grande Dame Rose. One he sat down next to Brandi, we all touched glasses in the middle, and date night was officially on. Things were smooth and chill as we sipped champagne while conversing with Devin and Lamar. We knew that sex was the reason we were there, but neither of them were pushing for it to begin, or seemed desperate to get their dicks wet. Lamar broke out an already rolled Slim-Jim sized blunt, fired it up, passed it to me, I toked it a few times, then passed it to Brandi. As the four-way conversation split into two individual conversations.

Lamar and I chatted for a while before the heat between us grew too hot to not want to feel the burn of the flames. He had my full attention as he spoke. The man was telling me something about one of his business ventures; but after a while, I heard his voice but not the words. I was too busy studying him to pay attention. He was sharp as a motherfucker. His shape up was perfect, as were his waves, mustache, and beard. The surface of his cocoa brown skin was smooth and looked healthy. My eyes focused on his lips. Watching them move as I took a hit on the joint, inhaled, and exhaled as I stopped myself from biting my own. His lips were beautiful. Full, juicy, and as I watched them in motion; I saw that his teeth were pearly white. He was wearing a dark blue, custom tailored button down with platinum and diamond cufflinks. I could see that beneath his shirt was the upper torso of a man that took care of his body. It was impossible to hide his muscular physique. This man was close to perfect as I've even seen. Devin was six-four and athletically built; while his friend was six-two, stocky, dark, handsome, and turning me the fuck on!

****

The suite had two large bedrooms. I led Lamar by the hand from the balcony to the first room and closed the door. No sooner than it shut, he was all over me. With the lights dimmed, making the atmosphere dark and romantic; he pinned me to the door from the back. I bit my lip and moaned a little as he pressed his body to mine. His dick against my ass. Separated by our clothing. I reached up and behind me, cupping the back of his head as his mouth found my neck. I gyrated my ass against him as he turned my face towards him and kissed me. Normally, I didn't kiss my dates. I let this one slide though. Lamar tasted good. His lips were as warm and soft as they looked. When he slid his tongue into my mouth, I accepted it. Sucking on it before giving him mine. He moved back some and slid his hand into my dress. Palming titty as his other hand slipped under my skirt. I kissed him harder as his fingers moved my thong to the side and began probing my clit and pussy lips.

He led me towards the bed, sat down on the edge of it, and standing in between his legs; I began to undress. Lamar stared up into my eyes as he unbuttoned his shirt. With my heels kicked off, I slid out of my dress as he undid his cufflinks and pulled his shirt off. Revealing his smooth cocoa- colored muscles, tattoos, and clean white tank top. Which he was pulling over his head as I removed my thong and tossed it. Now, I was only wearing my jewelry. I lowered down to my knees and began opening his belt and pants while staring up into his eyes. Lamar lifted his hips for me, I removed his slacks and underwear at the same time, then I took hold of his penis with one hand; his testicles with the other. I stared at his dick as I slowly stroked it. Softly massaging his scrotum at the same time. I licked my lips in anticipation, because this motherfucker had a beautiful package. At least nine inches of thickness and his sack was smooth and heavy. He put his hand on the back of my head as I lowered my face, opening my mouth at the same time.

I closed my eyes as I sucked his dick. Lamar kept his hand on the back of my head as I slowly took him deep into my mouth. Keeping my tongue flat and pressed against the underside of his shaft. The sound of his groans turned me on, causing me to grip his dick and balls even tighter as I sucked him harder. Covering his dick in my spit because my mouth was watering. With my pussy pulsing and throbbing, I looked up at Lamar as I held the base of his dick with both hands, slowly gliding my drool dripping tongue up the underside of his dick. When I reached the top, I kept my eyes locked on his lip biting, aggressively turned-on face as I swirled my tongue around the head of his penis, then wrapped my lips around it. Closing my eyes. Relaxing my throat. And roughly deep throating him in the blink of an eye. Lamar gripped my hair in his fist, growled like a bulldog, and his ass came up off the bed as I fought my gag reflex. With all but half an inch of his dick in my mouth.

Several wet and warm minutes later, Lamar made me stop sucking his dick before I made him cum. Which I knew he was close to doing. He stood up, roughly yanked me to my feet, then lied back on the bed; pulling me on top of him. He then moved me up his body so that he could suck on my titties. He held my waist as I moved from side to side, letting him suck, bite, and licked on my nipples; one at a time. He was aggressive and rough with his mouth, but that shit felt good. I had my eyes closed, enjoying having my titties sucked, when I heard the muffled sound of Brandi getting fucked in the other room. Devin suddenly had her moaning and screaming, *"HARDER!!"* I ignored her as Lamar moved me further up his body. I caught on to what he wanted and straddled his head. Putting my dripping wet pussy right in his face. I braced my hands on the bed above his head as he grabbed my ass and sucked on my clit. My mouth dropped open as Lamar ate my pussy something fierce.

He was really enjoying himself beneath me. He had me shaking and moaning like a motherfucker until I came. I was loud as fuck as my orgasm tore through me. He kept licking, sucking, and making noise as he pulled me down by my ass. I knew why he was so turned on. When I cum, my pussy gets super juicy. Apparently, that lights his fire. Because he didn't stop eating me out. Even after I came. Lamar roughly moved me onto my back, crawled on top of me, and without a condom on; he slid his dick into my waiting pussy. I clutched his shoulders and arched my back as he drove his dick all the way inside me. I was extra sensitive in the wake of my orgasm. He felt huge in my pussy and with each long, deep, and hard stroke; I was hit with hot shocks of pain and lightning bolts of pleasure. I lifted my head to watch him fuck me. I kept my knees bent and thighs opened wide; watching his dick sliding back & forth. Slick and gooey with my milky wetness. The wet sound of him fucking me was driving me wild and I started playing with my clit as he pounded his dick into me. Moaning just as hard as he was.

He didn't last very long in my wet tunnel. Lamar was coated in sweat and growling like a bear as hammered my pussy. He stroked away for about four minutes before he quickly pulled out. He was loud as he rapidly stroked his dick, shooting his nut in long streams onto my belly and both titties. I was propped up on my elbows, moaning with my mouth open as I watched him cum all over me. When he was done, he sat back and I dropped onto the bed. Both of us out of breath. We stayed like that for a minute, before I got up and made my way to the bathroom. I cleaned his semen off of me, peed, then turned on the shower and climbed in. Less than a minute later, Lamar joined me under the hot spray like I knew he would. Neither of us didn't say a word. We just started going at it again. I gave him head, then he fucked me from the back as the water jets soaked us. He came on my ass to end round two. Outside the shower, he put me up on the sink and ate my pussy again. Making me cum harder than the first time. We were done after that and he asked me to stay the night. He paid me $4000 and I was feeling him. Sleeping with him wasn't a hard decision for me.

Lamar and I smoked a little more weed in bed. Naked. As he lied on his back, I cuddled up to him like I was his lady. I lied my head on his shoulder and we talked and joked while I softly massaged his dick and balls. He fell asleep before I did and I lied there for a minute. Enjoying the quietness of the room and the rhythmic sound of his masculine breathing as he slept. For just a moment, I indulged a fantasy. That Lamar was my man and I was his woman. That he belonged to me. I belonged to him. I lied there caressing his penis with his strong and muscular arm around my shoulder; pretending that he & I were a couple in love. Though I didn't acknowledge it often; I was lonely. I dated a variety of men. For their pleasure and my financial security, but there was a part of me that craved something real. Affection. Adoration. To be treasured. Loved. As I felt sadness starting to bubble up to the surface; I checked myself. I shook off the fantasy that wasn't my reality. I reminded myself what was real and closed my eyes. At least I wasn't sleeping alone that night.

I made my money and got some bomb ass sex in the process. Increasing my cash flow was my goal. My ambition. My reality. Chasing love was a fantasy that I couldn't afford to pursue. It cost too much.

****

In the morning, I woke up to Lamar playing with my pussy. Rubbing my clit and fingering me. Once I had his fingers all warm and sticky, I rolled him onto his back and gave him a dick suck that curled his toes. This time when we fucked, he put on a condom. After we were done, as he went back to sleep, I got dressed and left him to rest. I met Brandi in the living room area and we departed together. She looked just as worn out as I did. Since we arrived in her car, she invited me over to her place to rest and chill. We stopped for coffee and breakfast, then drove over to her apartment. Her place was nice. Spacious, done mostly in white, and had a comforting atmosphere. We stripped down, B gave me one of her tank tops to sleep in, we smoked a cigarette with an early morning drink at her dining table as we regaled one another with our sexual tryst with the guys. Then it was time to get some much-needed sleep. Brandi and I climbed into her Queen-sized bed. Back-to-back, we were out within minutes.

When I opened my eyes, it wasn't the fact that it was the early evening that somewhat surprised me. It was my friend. Brandi was lying on her side like I was. Staring at me. I was somewhat taken aback that she had been lying there watching me sleep, but as I stared back at her; I couldn't look away. Her eyes motivated me to hold her stare. When a soft smile creased her lips, one formed on mine too. I figured out quickly why she was looking at me in such a way. I thought it was just me that felt it. A few times since we met, I had caught myself looking at her in a way I never looked at another female before. Intimately. Brandi was just as pretty as I was, but she looked more innocent than I did. Her features were softer. More youthful. We lied there for a while staring at each other, until she finally spoke. She whispered that she wanted to kiss me. Instead of telling her to go ahead, I gave her what she desired. What I desired. I moved closed to her, we put our hands on each other's cheek's, and softly pressed our lips together.

Kissing Brandi, tasting her, was the sweetest and warmest flavor that my mouth had ever experienced. Our kiss went from warm and soft, to hot and hard in the blink of an eye. We were all over each other. Kissing until it became hard to breathe. Our tongue danced, her hand palmed my ass cheek, and I slipped mine into her gown. Palming her titty. I had never been so hot for another human being before. Brandi and I stripped what little clothing we had on and it was nothing but fire from there. We pleased each other's breasts, massaged one another's clit, fingered each other, and then we made one another orgasm. Multiple times. I ate her pussy, she ate mine, and then took turns using her vibrator. By the time Brandi and I ran out of gas; it was getting dark out. We smoked in her bed with some music on, sipped wine as we talked. Later on, after we showered together *(going at it again)*, we ordered Chinese and relaxed on her couch for the rest of the night. I didn't know shit about being with another woman, but B seemed to be comfortable with me being the dominant partner.

She lied in between my legs, with the back of her head against my chest as we reclined on the couch. She was sipping on a glass of wine and I was smoking a cigarette as we watched a new episode of Power on Starz. She was Team Ghost and I was Team Kanan. B had a serious crush in Omari Hardwick; I was in love with 50 Cent. That was how our night went. We chilled in each other's embrace binge watching shows, talking about different shit, laughing a bit as we joked, smoked more weed, and then we went to bed around one am. I spent the night with Brandi and we slept together like lovers. Which we obviously were now. She lied on her side in front of me with my arm around her. Our legs intertwined and the top of her head under my chin. It felt so good to be lie like this. The last time I felt this warm, safe, and at ease; I was with Raheem. Now, it was Brandi in my life to make me feel this way. Comfortable. Able to smile. Adored. No longer alone.

About five weeks after our date with Devin & Lamar, my dark chocolate lover from that night hit me up. The last time he messaged me was after he returned to LA. He hit my inbox to tell me that he enjoyed our night together. I replied, telling him that I did as well. We sort of talked about maybe seeing one another again, but he informed me that he will let me know. He and his homie had business coming up that was going to keep them busy for a minute. The same night, Lamar hit my DM. Brandi was out on a date with one of her regulars. An older brother that owned a luxury car dealership. My girl's client was a trip. He paid her a thousand dollars for five, sometimes ten minutes of sex. He was a cute forty-five-year-old man with a wife and three grown kids that was successful, lived well, and was a man of supreme confidence. Despite having a four-and-a-half-inch penis and came very quickly. B had me dying laughing as she told me that half the time, he sometimes nutted after less than two minutes of getting head and had nothing left to fuck.

While Brandi was entertaining her client, I was taking a break. I made close to ten-grand in just under a week. I decided to take a few days to myself. I normally stayed in or went somewhere with B. That night, I decided to go have some fun. Regular people fun. I threw on a pair of tight-ripped front blue jeans, a new pair of J's, a tight-fitting white T-shirt, then grabbed my varsity jacket and purse on my way out the door. I parked in a well-lit four-story garage and decided to walk the strip. I strolled amongst everyone else out for a night in Vegas. My first stop was a fast- food joint that was a thousand times better than McDonald's or Burger King. I enjoyed a delicious double quarter pound Texas style

Black Angus cheeseburger with bacon-cheddar chilli fries and a vanilla milkshake. From there, I made my way to an arcade. I played a couple shooter games, a sit on motorcycle machine, then I burned through ten dollars in quarters playing Street Fighter II and Mortal Kombat 3 . From the arcade, I swayed my juicy ass over to the casino at Caesar's Palace.

I won $200 on the quarter slots, won & lost money playing roulette, and had a fun ass time at the craps table. I had a hot hand for a minute. People were cheering for me and shit. After winning $8,000 on a roll; I decided to cash out. I took my chips to the window with one of the burgundy suit-jacket wearing security guys as an escort. I smiled as I accepted my clean, banded stack of cash. The security dude walked me through the casino and I tipped him as I left. He was with me until I exited the Palace to make sure that I didn't robbed while on Caesar's property. I walked to another hotel, but I was done with gambling for the evening. I won some money, had fun, and now I just wanted to fall back and chill before I went home. I found a laid back, Jazz style bar and went inside. With my vodka & cranberry, plus my cigarettes. I sat in the back by myself in a booth and zoned out. Live Jazz musicians & soul singers took the stage to provide the perfect musical vibe that I needed to relax. When my phone screen on the table lit up, I checked it to see what it was.

A DM notification from Lamar. I was anticipating that it was him hitting me up to establish a date for us to hook up again. It was, but not like before. His message was an invitation. For me and Brandi to come to LA to meet a friend of his. A friend that was in the adult film industry. Lamar told me to call him at my earlier convenience for more details. I sat back with my cigarette and thought about it. Hmmmm?? The adult film industry. Porn. Getting into the porno bizz never crossed my mind. One of my clients had told me one night that I should be in porn movies, but I brushed it off. I made pop a nut in three minutes giving him head and just before I left his hotel room that night; he suggested that I should seriously look into doing porn. Now, my four-thousand-dollar date was offering to connect me with a friend that makes X-rated films. I wasn't turned off or offended by the offer; but I wasn't about to dive in head first either. I left the bar, made my way back to the garage, and as I was driving home; I called Lamar.

I listened as he kept it real with me. The sexual encounter he had with me was pure fire. He told me that I was one of the best he had ever been with. I was smiling as I drove. Feeling my ego inflate a little. Lamar joked about us fucking again, but then he elaborated on the offer. He asked me if I ever heard of Bryan Powers? I thought about the name and then it hit me. I told Lamar that I did. He started High Power Productions. An indie porn company that exclusively featured black actors and actresses. I added in that I downloaded some of their videos. Lamar shared with me that he, Devin, and Bryan Powers grew up together. They helped their homie build his company after he got out of prison. They gave him the start-up money. Since then, HPP was on the top indie labels in LA. Ok, I stated. Then I asked Lamar what did that have to do with me and Brandi? I kind of knew, but I just wanted to hear him say it. Bryan heard about my girl and I from his childhood friends. Bryan Powers knew who were, certainly what we looked like, and it was clear as day that he knew all about our sexual forte.

The indie porn mogul, through his home boys, was inviting B and I out to LA to meet and greet to discuss joining his company. I was intrigued by the offer, but I wanted to talk it over with my girl first. Thus, I told Lamar that I will get back to him. ASAP. I drove home to wait for Brandi to return from her date. She came in just after four am. I was still awake. Lying on the bed watching TV in just my panties. I had showered, ordered food, and smoked as I waited up for her. I let her get settled down and in bed with me before I told her about my conversation with Lamar. The invitation and offer from Bryan Powers. B was all for it. She revealed to me that she thought about doing porno, but never pursued it. I informed her that I was down. I heard that the porno world was wild, but the top-chicks made serious money once their name started ringing out and their popularity soared. I was confident that once them horny motherfuckers got a load of me and Brandi, we were going to be a big hit.

I messaged Lamar before B crawled on top of me and we started kissing and touching each other. I informed him that we were game. Waiting for the details on travelling to Los Angeles. Though I was intrigued by the money, I was excited by the prospect of becoming a star in the adult film industry. Sex is something I'm good at. Very good at. I had motherfuckers in Vegas and other cities hooked on my body and sexual skills as if I was drug. I pleased men better than their damn wives. I'm able to turn a man on without saying a word. Once they're in my hands; I melt their ass like butter. As B ate my pussy, I imagined making serious money doing it on camera. I wasn't scared or nervous. This is what I do. What I am. I am the fire. I am seduction. At twenty-years old, I was the living personification of pleasure & lust. I'm a bad bitch.

Everyone was about to find out why.

CHAPTER SEVEN

"Wet, Willing, Warm, and Wild."

Los Angeles was sexier in real life than it looked on TV and in the movies. Brandi & I were going to drive from Nevada to California. That was the plan until Devin & Lamar intervened. It was nearly a four-hour drive from Vegas to LA. Before we even had a chance to hit the road, Lamar called me and asked for our information. Less than an hour later, he emailed me the confirmation receipts for two first-class seats on JetBlue airways. B & I took a Lyft to the airport, checked in, went through security, and found a seat at our gate. As we waited for our flight, we did our own thing. Brandi had her earbuds in. Listening to music as she looked at shoes and clothes. I also had my buds in. Watching messy-ratchet videos on Instagram. My chick was nodding her head as she switched to scrolling Facebook. Thirty-five minutes after we arrived in the waiting area; our plane was at the gate. I tapped Brandi, we picked up our bags, and when first-class passengers were announced over the speakers, we boarded.

My first time on an airplane was both scary and exciting. Brandi and I spent the hour and twenty five-minute flight having a little fun. We took cute pics together, Snap-filter selfies, then I browsed websites for shoes & outfits. I bought a pair of Christian Dior wrap around stilettos, a pair of white & powder pink Jordan XII's (Twelves), along with a matching three-piece Jordan jogging-track suit. I bought the same sneakers and outfit for Brandi. Only hers was white & powder blue. We boarded the plane at 8:10 am. At 9:40, the flight attendant announced that we were five minutes from landing at LAX international Airport. To please de-activate all Bluetooth features on all of our devices, please return our seats to their normal upright positions, and to please fasten our seatbelts. She finished by thanking us for flying with JetBlue airways, welcome to Los Angeles California, and to enjoy our time in the City of Angels.

Waiting for us at the gate with our last names on a white poster board was a twenty-something year old dude in a white button down and slacks. He was clean cut and polite as he greeted us, then asked Brandi and I to follow him. We were led through the terminal and outside to a waiting White Lincoln Navigator. De'Andre, our driver, opened the rear hatch, put our bags inside, then held the door open for us, helped us climb in, and then he got behind the wheel and off we went. Brandi and I were all smiles and excitement as we watched LA pass by. It was like the world was whole different kind of brightness. The vast colors of California's environment were vibrant. OMG! There were palm trees everywhere! De'Andre was the perfect chaperone. He answered all of our questions, told us things about LA, and dropped a few names of restaurants we should hit while we were in town. An hour after we landed, the SUV rolled to a stop in the winding driveway of a beautiful residence.

It was a one level mansion and we had to be at least a quarter mile from the main road. There were a dozen luxury cars and SUV's parked in front of the place. De'Andre told us that our bags were good in the Navigator as held the door open for us. B and I followed him up the smooth stone stairs and into the house. There was some kind of party going on. People were everywhere. In the living room, dining room, and because of the many floor to ceiling windows; I could see people outside. On the deck and around the pool. A few people were swimming too. As we followed our chaperone, I studied everyone having a good time. Most of the niggas were shirtless, various shades of brown, and all of them looked good! I saw muscles of different forms, tattoo's, beards, dreads, sharp cuts, and shiny jewelry. The women partying with those niggas may have had on bikini's, but they might as well had been naked. I saw various sized titties and asses. Just like the men, the women varied in appearance as well.

There wasn't a chick below an eight rating in attendance. I saw nothing but pretty, sexy, and cute females all over the place. Some were dark, others were light, a few were caramel, a couple were honey toned, and I saw one sitting on a niggas lap on the deck, giving homie a lap dance. She was fucking gorgeous! She had long, streaked blond hair, medium brown colored skin, the juiciest lips, more ass than a stallion, and she looked exotic. I guessed she was part Black and part Asian. De'andre led us to a large room where the master of the house was waiting for us. Devin and Lamar were sitting around a glass dining table with the man that we were here to see. Bryan Powers. Being gentlemen, when we were escorted into the room, they stood up and welcomed us to California. We did the hug and smile thing with the men we knew, then B & I were introduced to the man we didn't yet know. Brandi was closer to him, so Bryan shook her hand first. I stood just off to her side, admiring him as if he was glowing.

The night Lamar told me about Mr. Powers, I looked him up online. I had heard of him, but had never seen him before. When his picture filled my phone screen, all I could think was, "DAMN!" Bryan Powers was one sexy ass man! Beautiful to be more accurate. He stood six-foot three, was nothing but muscle, he wore his hair short with perfect waves and a fade, his beard was exquisitely trimmed & groomed, and his brown skin looked like smooth milk chocolate. He was laying the charm on my girl, but it wasn't his voice that had me. It was his eyes and his smile. The man had light brown eyes and his teeth looked like a different kind of white. When he turned his focus on me, my smile was ear to ear as we shook hands. He was looking right into my eyes as he welcomed me to Cali, stated that it was pleasure to meet me. After he shook my hand; he kissed the back of it. I immediately noted that he didn't do that to Brandi.

Devin and Lamar left us with Bryan as they went to join the party. One of the bad chicks in a bikini joined. She was introduced as Nya, and Bryan asked us what we would like to drink? Brandi requested a Gin & Lime, a Grey Goose Vodka & OJ for me. We made small talk with Bryan until our drinks arrived. Once Nya and her jiggling ass cheeks departed; we got down to it. The black porn mogul was polite, but direct with us. He asked were we sure about wanting to do porn? Before either B or I replied, he issued a subtle warning. By telling us that this life wasn't for everyone. Especially females. Ninety percent of the chicks that tried to get in on the porn scene didn't make the cut. Professional fucking & sucking on camera wasn't for them. It was too much. They couldn't deal with the pressure, function with so many eyes on them, or they weren't as freaky, confident, or open with their sexuality as they thought they were. B and I looked at one another for a moment. Feeling bold, I looked at Bryan and gave it to him straight.

I told him that we knew what we were getting into. Pleasing a man, or a woman, was nothing new to us. He studied me with his hands folded on the table as I spoke; but his pretty eyed, penetrating stare didn't phase me. I went on to say that I knew that we had a lot to learn about this business, how to work in it, and though we were more than willing to listen and learn; neither of us was scared or nervous. All due respect, that timid shit was for little girls. We were grown women. Bryan nodded his head with a relaxed smirk. He asked Brandi was she on the same page and she replied back with a confident yes. He nodded again, checked his watch, and then shared his thoughts. He explained that he liked our look, he was feeling our swag, and he was going to see how we got down. In person. For the time being though, he wanted us to enjoy ourselves. Meet his people, get some food, and have a good time. Brandi and I followed Bryan from the dining room to the deck. Meeting people all the way there. We shook hands and hugged more than a dozen of our soon to be co-workers.

For the rest of the morning and afternoon, it was nothing but fun for us. Brandi and I conversed with dudes and chicks that we both seen and have never seen in adult films. Everyone was welcoming, friendly, inviting, and cool. We laughed at jokes, shared a few personal facts with them, sipped drinks, a bad ass redbone named Kiana Green fired up some bomb ass haze and we got lit. Then we sat down at one of the umbrella tables to eat. Around four pm, most of them had left the mansion. Devin and Lamar were kicking it with us near the pool. We were engaged in a four-way conversation as we chilled. I was smoking a cigarette, laughing at Lamar's story when De'Andre walked up. He informed B and I that he was taking us to where we were staying. Bryan set up a spot for us and he wanted us to head over there, clean up, and rest a little before he picked us up again that night. An hour and a half later, Brandi and I were in a hotel room. A fairly large suite at the Radisson. We got out something to wear, took a shower together, and then left a few of the windows open as we cuddled up for a nap. Brandi and I fell asleep face to face.

****

I decided to be ready for what I knew was coming. When De'Andre called to say that he was in front of the hotel, I exited the front doors with Brandi. Dressed for the occasion. She went with a tank top, tiny shorts, and her sandals. I had on a tight, form fitting, short sleeved plaid pattern top, a pair of equally tight jeans, and three-inch heels. My hair was pulled back in a low pony tail and I had no underwear on. No bra or panties. De'Andre pulled off after helping us climb into his vehicle. The drive was only twenty-minutes. We arrived in a quiet neighborhood, parking in front of a house that was surrounded by tall brick & stone wall with an automatic gate. Once in the house, it was just like when we arrived at the mansion. There were mad people in attendance, but the vibe was totally different. The same people we saw at the party were now in work mode. Dudes and chicks were sitting around the living and dining room in robes, shorts, their underwear, and some chicks only had their panties on. Titties out with no shame.

De'Andre introduced us to a pretty as fuck brown skin chick named Tia. She had smallish titties under a black tank top, but a monster ass covered by white yoga pants. She was all smiles as friendliness as she asked me and Brandi to come with her. She led us up the stairs to a huge bedroom. Inside of it was nothing but a king-sized bed and four people. Bryan Powers, a light skinned dude with dreads holding a digital camera, and two muscled out niggas. They were laughing and joking when we came in. Bryan greeted us, introduced us to his homies, then asked us were we ready? Both Brandi and I nodded our heads. He looked at the caramel- colored brother with the ripped, covered in tats body. He pointed at Brandi as he informed his actor that she was his. Dude was polite as he stepped up to my girl, gently took her by the hand, and escorted her towards the bed. There were two photo shoot lights set up and focused on the bed area. Bryan guided us to the back of the room and I watched B get initiated into porn.

The dude she was with went by the name D.C. Brown. He sat Brandi on the edge of the bed, stood over top of her, and as he untied the draw string of his sweatpants, he calmly asked her to take her top off. She did as she was told while looking up at him. She tossed her tank top and looked down at the dick in front of her. Being stroked. D.C. was blessed. His pipe was about eight inches long, veiny, and slightly curved upwards. He stopped stroking it as he moved forward and B didn't need to be told what to do next. She took hold of his dick and balls. Stroking and massaging it as the camera man moved in closer. To record at different angles. I stood in between Bryan and my partner. A damn giant. I watched Brandi take ol' boy's dick in her mouth, then I checked out the nigga I was going to shoot my first scene with. His name was Victor. He had to be six-five and built like a pro wrestler. He seemed cool, but he looked like a nigga that spent quite a bit of time in prison. I mean the motherfucker had muscles all over, his hands were huge, and when I looked down at his print through his basketball shorts; I saw that he was packing a monster down there.

D.C. put it on my girl something vicious. After she sucked his dick for a good while, as her saliva dripped from it, he returned the favor. He moved her back onto the bed, pulled her shorts off, sucked and licked on her titties for a bit, then moved his face between her legs. From where I stood, he definitely knew what he was doing. His lips, fingers, and tongue had Brandi feeling good. She moaned non-stop, pulled his head in deeper, rotated her hips, and the nigga made her cum. Hard. Before she could even recover, the camera man tossed his homie a rubber. He quickly put it on and penetrated her. Roughly. I watched her get fucked hard and fast for the next eleven minutes. D.C. dicked her down missionary with her legs spread wide, up on his shoulders, from the side, and doggy style. It was when he was banging her out doggy with her head pulled back, making her moan and scream that I broke my trance. Realizing that my pussy was dripping wet and my nipples were hard as rocks. Watching my girl get fucked the way she was turned me on like never before.

Brandi's initiation scene came to an end when D.C. unleashed his money shot. He and B were fucking hard and fast on the edge of the bed. Both of them were covered in sweat, her eyes were barely open, and her titties were bouncing up and down as he slammed his dick into her. When he was ready to nut, he quickly pulled out, moving forward as he removed the condom. With a handful of her hair, he rapidly stroked his dick in front of her face as he shot his cum all over it. I bit my lip and tried to rub my pussy with my thighs as I watched several streams of semen shoot out of D.C.'s dick. Landing on B's cheek, up her forehead, across her lips, and onto her outstretched tongue. D.C. was growling & laughing as he looked into the camera. Telling the recording lens how much he loved redbone pussy! The camera man then focused on Brandi and her semen-streaked smiling face as she licked his dripping dick, sucked it a little, and then gave the head a big wet kiss.

Bryan smirked, telling her she did good as the camera man snapped a few pictures of her with a regular camera. Tia returned at the King's call. She was instructed to take Brandi to clean up, then see to it that she gets something to eat and is comfortable. Tia was all smiles as she chewed her gum, taking Brandi by the hand and leading her and D.C out of the room. The camera man was getting his gear ready as Bryan looked at me. Grinning as told me that I was up. Victor took my hand and I went with him towards the bed. Unlike my girl, I didn't let my partner lead. I wanted to impress Bryan and make a damn good first impression. I crawled onto the bed, turned on my knees, and as Victor was untying his shorts, the camera man informed his boss that he was rolling. I didn't focus on anything other than the nigga in front of me. Vic and I were in a hot stare down as he took his shorts off and I was unbuttoning my top. I left it on as I unsnapped my jeans and pulled the zipper down. I moved to the edge of the bed, taking in Victor's anaconda as I moved in position to suck it.

Fuck, his dick was huge! There was at least nine and a half inches of massive penis in front of me. Not only was it long, it was thick AF! I saw a real challenge in the head I wanted to give him, but I was up for it. He was slow, long stroking it as he stood in front of me. Still looking up at him, I gave him a little tongue slow swiping my lips action as I indicated for him to come to me. With a devilish grin on his face, he complied. I took hold of his dick as soon as he was in range. It felt so big and heavy in my hand as I stroked it. I stared at it as I cupped his balls. Firmly. As Victor placed his hand on the back of my head, I glanced over at Bryan. He was leaning against the wall with his arms crossed. Intently watching us. Seeing that lustful look in his eyes turned me on even more. I licked my lips for him, then returned my attention to Victor as I wrapped them around the head of his dick.

I moaned and he groaned as I took more than half of his nine inches into my mouth. I controlled my gag reflex and kept going. Squeezing his balls with my closed my eyes. Trying to bury my nose in his pubic hair. Victor had a fist of my hair as I pulled my head back. Drool spilled from my bottom lip as Victor pulled his dick out of my mouth. It was slick with my spit. He then moved me back on the bed, roughly pulled my jeans off, and then buried his face between my legs. As I ran my nails over his bald head, I first looked at the camera man. He was close to the bed and I stared into the lens focused on me as I moaned, bit my lip, and then licked them. Victor ate me out with an aggressive eagerness. Like every dude that ate my pussy. He was loving how wet and juicy I got. I was enjoying Victor's long, fat tongue inside me as I shifted my gaze to Bryan. To my subtle surprise, he was doing more than just watching us. He had taken his shirt off and undid his jeans. He had stood there with his dick out. Slowly stroking it as he watched.

Victor made me cum. Hard and loud. With his tongue swirling on my clit, two of his huge fingers in my pussy, and one in my anus. He finger fucked the hell out me as he ate me. Making me shake, twist, and damn near squirt. His fingers were slick and gooey. Compelling him to tell the camera how much he was loving my pussy. It was so fuckin' juicy! After I came, I thought the was going to put a condom on; but he slid in raw. Groaning in ecstasy at how wet, hot, and tight I was. With my shirt open and titties exposed, he held my legs opened wide as he fucked me. In long, deep strokes. Coating his dick with my nectar, unable to stop announcing how wet my pussy was. As he started stroking hard and faster, I looked at Bryan again. He was still beating his dick. Only more vigorously now. I was so fuckin' turned on! Victor was hittin' deep.

Though his dick felt absolutely delicious inside me; I wanted more. I told Bryan to join in with my eyes as I moaned.

Vic moved me into the doggy style position, with Bryan lying on his back underneath me. He guided my head as I feverishly sucked his dick. Victor put a death grip on my hips as he long dicked me. He was hitting my G-spot and my pussy loudly squished with each thrust. Bryan was growling through clenched teeth as I deep throated him. I had his genitals covered in saliva as I stared right into his eyes. All three of us were making noise. Vic was going so hard & deep that his thighs were slapping into my ass with a loud thwack with every stroke. My entire body was shivering and shaking because getting fucked like this felt so fucking good!! Even more so with Bryan's dick in my throat. I had his entire package drenched. He roughly guided my head as Vic was going all in on me. I didn't stop sucking or take my eyes off of Bryan as the big nigga beating up my pussy called out that he was cumming. I was milking the dick in my mouth as I felt Victor's hot nut shooting onto my ass cheeks. I started making them jiggle as Bryan announced that he was nuttin' too. He forced his dick into my throat as he pushed my head down on it. He started fucking my mouth as he came. I didn't look away from him or the camera behind him as I swallowed shot after shot of his warm vanilla milkshake.

****

Miss Tia came for me after Bryan and Victor finished telling how lit the scene we just did was. I smiled and acted all cute; ignoring how I was. There was cum on my ass cheeks, my hair was fucked up, my inner thighs were all creamy, and my chest was covered in drying saliva. The men that ran a train on me were amped up. Excitedly raving about how dope I was. I was standing in between them, the camera man was still recording, and Vic started playing with my titties as he looked at Bryan. Informing him that he definitely wanted to shoot a scene with me again. I couldn't stop smiling. Both of them were fondling me when Tia opened the door. Vic was still toying with my nipples, while Bryan had his hand between my legs. Gently stroking my still wet pussy. Tia was laughing as she pried me away from them and escorted me down the hall to a bathroom. She gave me a clean towel & wash cloth, then informed me that there was a bathrobe hanging on the back of the bathroom door for me.

After taking a nice and long hot shower, scrubbing myself clean, I dried off and made my way downstairs. I passed by rooms where the sounds of fucking were on the other side of the door. I found Brandi sitting in the living room. She was on a sofa with a pretty brown skinned chick in a robe like us. They were talking and drinking when I came down. I got myself a beer and the chick gave up her seat so that I could sit with my girl. Everyone was relaxed and chilling. Some were watching TV, texting, looking at something on their phone, or engaged in conversation. By four in the morning, Bryan wrapped things up. All of the scenes were shot and it was time to get paid. As everyone was leaving, Tia handed them a white envelope. Brandi and I were the last to depart. We had changed back into what we had on when we arrived. As De'Andre drove us back to our hotel, we opened up the envelopes. There was $500 in Brandi's, $800 in mine. Neither of us said anything about the difference in what we were paid, but I knew why I was given more. I fucked two niggas at once, plus Bryan was more impressed by my performance than he was with my girls set. B didn't seem at all jealous or mad. We shared our money anyway. Our first shoot in the business netted us $1300. A good nights' work if you ask me.

Brandi and I slept until the mid afternoon after De'Andre dropped us off. I was up first. As I was standing at the window looking out at LA and smoking a cigarette, I heard a notification go off on my phone. I retrieved it from the night table on my side of the bed and unlocked the screen. It was a video file message from Bryan. I hit play. It was the recording from the previous night. The video was HD quality. I watched myself getting fucked by Victor as I sucked Bryan's dick. The video was edited & cut down to three and a half minutes. A lot was trimmed out to only show the highlight moments of the entire session. I was grinning to myself as I watched streams of nut shoot onto my jiggling ass cheeks, then a close up of my face as Bryan came in my mouth. The clip ended with me smiling with my shirt open, hair wild, face lightly coated in sweat, and my lips, neck, and titties wet with saliva. Bryan sent a text message with the video.

"You're a natural, baby girl…My inner circle love your look and your skills…Your girl did good too and I'm working on ya'll contracts…you gonna be big in the game, boo!…Rest and relax…I'll hit you back when the contracts are ready."

I woke Brandi up to tell her the news. We were in the game now. The porno game. B was just as excited as I was. I envisioned us making big money, becoming popular porn stars, and living a life of luxury, fun, and hot sex. I was a bad as fuck young bitch with a gold mine between my legs. They say that sex sells. I planned to make a killing selling it. Not only was I beautiful, I felt that I was at the top of my game when it came to sexual pleasure. All of those horny motherfuckers out there were going to fall in love with my ass! Yeah. I was a bad bitch indeed. I was going to get paid! To celebrate, Brandi and I got wild in our hotel room. We made a quick run for some liquor, fired up some weed, got freaky, and ended up in the shower. Surrounded by steam as we kissed, sucked & licked each other's titties, fingered one another, and then ate one another out before chilling for the rest of the day.

Bae' and I ended up falling asleep on the couch with the TV on. Naked and comfortable. We made a promise as we lied there watching a movie. We promised to stay loyal to one another. No matter who we fucked on camera or chilled with when not shooting; no nigga or bitch would come between us. We promised one another to never allow this business we were going into to compromise our bond. That it was me & her. No matter what. Brandi confessed her love to me, I reciprocated, we kissed, and then settled in to finish our movie and get some sleep. Bryan texted me after Brandi fell out. Our contracts were drawn up and ready to be reviewed and signed. He added that a lawyer will be present to go over them with us. To explain all the details of what we'll be signing. The text ended with him telling me that De'Andre will be here to pick us up in the morning.

Tomorrow will be my official day in my quest to become a porn star.

CHAPTER EIGHT

*"L.A. told me, you'll be a rock star / All you have to change /
Is everything you are."*

-Pink

Nine-months after I signed the contract with Bryan's adult films production company, I was a fabrication of my natural self. My true identity, my true self was buried under the lie he built me as. Not only my name, but how the world knew me when he made me public as one his new, hottest, and freakiest young stars. My biography profile on the High- Power Productions site listed my name as Tamani Taylor. Aka, Tamani Black. My bio said that I was eighteen and hailed from Gary, Indiana. The day that I signed the contract; two things happened. First, I was presented with a sign on check in the amount of $18,500. Second, I was immediately sent away to begin my make over. Which lasted for five days. The first step was meeting with an image & style consultant that worked for the company. Brandi had her own. My lady looked me over, studied me like a model-specimen, and then decided what my exterior image will be. The first thing she did was have my hair changed.

It was cut, dyed, and styled into a look I never went with. I went from having long brown hair, to a just above my shoulders jet-black bob style. With lavender colored streaks & highlights. The next change was my eyes. My consultant took me to visit an optometrist. To have colored contacts made. I went from light brown eyes to a weird ass color. Pale violet. I now had purple streaks in my hair and purple eyes. On day two, the pretty but robotic consultant brought in a body & fitness expert to assess my form. I was measured and analyzed, poked and prodded; then they came up with a workout routine for me. I was to focus most of my exercise routine on my abs, obliques, butt, and thighs. According to the assessment, my tits were perfect. 34D's. They were beautifully shaped, firm, and I had good sized nipples with large cocoa brown areolas. One thing was added to my breasts. The consultant had my right nipple pierced with a silver barbell. I was given a very long speech about hair & skin care, makeup, consistently pampering my nails, then there was the added visual flair they believed would make me stand out even more.

For two days, I spent most of each day in a tattoo shop. Getting ink on the left side of my frame. My shoulder down to my elbow, along my ribs from the side of my titty to my hip, and wrapping around onto my ass cheek was an exquisite display of various tats. Some had color, most were black, and I didn't decide what the tats would be. My consultant did. I offered no words of objection or resistance. I was a rookie at this. I let Bryan and the consultant do their work on me. Brandi's make over was different from mine. They didn't cut her hair. They extended it with sew ins. Her hair was now a blondish color and to the middle of her back. Her contacts were grey and I went with her to a doctors' office in Culver City. For a breast augmentation surgery. She was going from 36D to 40DD. Bryan decided that she'll be the sexy redbone with huge titties and an anal sex loving hottie; while I was the pretty & bad, booty poppin', DSL (Dick Sucking Lips) ebony star.

Being that B and I arrived on the scene with our own cash, we combined our signing money and got ourselves a nice ass apartment. It was an open floor plan, loft-studio close to Pasadena. We caught a plane back to Vegas, packed up our old place, sold her car, and then departed Nevada for good. We didn't even tell our landlord that we were leaving. We just bounced. A day after getting our stuff moved into our new place, Tia hit my phone. To run down the schedule that was put together for us. The next morning at seven am, our day long photo shoot began. Stylists did our hair and makeup, followed by wardrobe, and then we got to it. Brandi and I took turns posing solo in various sexy outfits & hair styles until noon. After lunch, we posed together. For our first session, we were in basketball jersey dresses, then in different bra & panty sets; followed by just thongs; then we shot completely naked. Most of our poses were subtle, while more than a few were hot & intimate. That came easy to us. We were already lovers.

I was tired as fuck by the time we arrived home. It was 12:03 am when B and I crashed on the bed. All day long it, was shoot after shoot at three different locations. Going through hair & makeup with each outfit-scene change. Our last shoot was in a suite at the Westin Hotel. Brandi was in another room as I was in mine with one of the male actors from HPP. It was a black lingerie themed session. He and I pretended to be lovers for a dozen poses; then it got hot. Pictures were taken of him sucking on my tit, of me stroking his dick, me laying on my back giving the camera a pleased look as he licked my pussy, me with his balls in my mouth, and they took a lot of pics of him fucking me. We weren't shooting a full scene, but the photographer got in close to snap photos of his dick sliding in and out of my pussy as I spread it open for him. The shoot ended after I gave him head to make him cum. All over my face and titties. I gave the camera a big smile with streaks of warm milky cum all over me.

Time began flying by. Week after week, I shot three to five scenes. At first, it was just boy-girl sessions. I partnered up with one of the dudes from the team and we shot our scene. Most times, it was just normal, choreographed sex. Dick sucking, pussy eating, 69, my partner slid his dick between my titties for a while, and then we fucked. Because my face and ass were my best assets, I gave a lot of wet-sloppy head, got fucked doggy style a lot, and my ass received a lot of time with the camera as I was always instructed to ride my scene partners. In a month, I shot fifteen scenes and Bryan picked three to add to my first video featurette. FRESH EBONY DIVA'S Vol. SIX. I had the first, fourth, and seventh scene on the playlist. Each one was with a different dude. Before the full-length video was released, ninety seconds of clips from each scene were uploaded to our web site. Within a day, all of my clips were trending. The view counter was clocking hits like a stopwatch and the comments were rolling in. All day long! Motherfuckers were on me!

Smut loving dudes all over the map were talking about Tamani Black. The new girl on the porn scene. The hot & sexy, sweet faced ebony with the beautiful titties, gorgeous skin tone, the prettiest ass, and the wettest pussy ever! That was my ace in hole. My pussy. She was a waterfall in every damn scene and the fan boys were loving it. One dude commented under my clip that I was his new favorite porn star and my pretty, honey dripping pussy had him beating his dick. 24-7. When the DVD and MP4 video streaming file were released, it was selling and being downloaded like brand-new J's. My pics on the site were being viewed, downloaded and shared too. Bryan wanted to capitalize on the wave, so he had me give the perv fan boys a special treat. For an entrance fee of $9.99, they got to see me on a LIVE stream as I put on a tease & please show for their masturbating joy. I was dressed in a see-thru white baby doll nighty and I gave them a solo set. I talked dirty to the web cam as I played with my titties, then my pussy, sucked on a nipples, jiggled my ass, and then made myself cum with a toy. The live stream ended with me licking my juices off of a nine-inch dildo.

Brandi was hot too. Horny ass men were loving her. She was doing boy-girl scenes, threesomes with two men, and she shot a very hot, anal heavy gangbang. Three dudes all took turns fucking her mouth, tits, pussy, and ass. I was there for that shoot. I creamed just watching my girl do her thing. She was loud and aggressive as them dudes gave it to her. By the time she was done with the last nigga, she looked like a wild, sexy animal. Covered in sweat and semen with her hair messed up and matted to her face. Within six months, my bae' and I were doing so well as newcomers; our numbers kept earning us pay bumps. When we started, Bryan was paying us $650 a scene. By the end of our third month; $800 a scene. After six months, we met with him to re-negotiate our scene rate and walked out of the meeting with a whole new pay level. Brandi was going to be making an even thousand dollars for every scene she shot, while I was going to receive $1500. My trending numbers were higher than hers. It was good business to pay me more. I was also awarded an additional benefit that I kept from my girl.

Bryan and I were seeing each other behind the scenes. When he was around and we were working; we kept it to business. He was no more friendly or hard on me than he was with anyone else. Bry was a cool ass dude for the most part though. He was funny, his mind was full of wisdom & intellect, he was fun to be around, and he seemed genuine about making sure that everyone under his brand was comfortable and happy. However, when it came to putting out money to produce high-quality material; he was like a drill sergeant. He didn't tolerate bullshit, excuses, internal beefs, or anyone not following his word and law when we were making films under his company's name. High Power was one of the top independent black adult film producers in Cali and competition was a bloodsport. The powerhouse brands were on top of the porn mountain and we were one of the few that was making them take notice. Thus, when Bryan was in the house as we were shooting our scenes; everyone was expected to be on their A-game.

That included me. His secret girlfriend. Both Brandi and I made friends with some of our teammates, so we started being together less and less. Though we were still in a relationship, we had begun doing our own thing away from one another. She became the fourth member of BTB. The Big Titty Bitches. Four chicks with double-D's and up. They loved to go out and get wild at the bars and clubs. I kicked it with a few of the girls, but most of my free time was spent with my man. Bryan was different when it was just the two of us. The house in Thousand Oaks where I met him was his actual home. I loved spending time with him. He was so much more relaxed, silly, and very, very affectionate. We were always kissing, cuddling, being intimate, and we fucked. All the time. He knew that I was free of STD's, because testing every 60-days was mandatory for all of us. Bryan and I didn't use condoms. He was the only man that busted his nut inside me. He didn't want kids, so he had a vasectomy long before we met. I didn't want kids either. Hence, I was on birth control.

I had the kind of love with Bryan that so damn comfortable. We didn't argue, fight, get mad, jealous, and there was never any toxicity between us. Shit, he fucked me behind-the-scenes with some of his boys, and I tag team sucked his dick with a few of the girls. Our people caught on that we were seeing each other outside of work, but everyone was cool with it. Brandi was doing the same thing. She and Victor had a thing going on. The difference was the two of them were off balance. Sexually, they had the perfect chemistry. Both on and off camera. B told me that she was hooked on his dick, like he was on her pussy. They claimed to be deeply in love. At first, I believed them. Seeing them together was like seeing a couple that was madly in love and been together for years. They looked at one another in that special way, were always hugged up at our parties and get together's, they loved their just the two of them hang out time, and they tatted each other's name on their body.

However, I knew from my bae' that the sugar between them wasn't always sweet. Time to time, their whole vibe was bitter as salt. Brandi and Victor were way too much alike. One minute, they were as nice as a puppy. Then in the blink of an eye, they were as vicious as a wolf. Both of them were emotional. Prone to become blinded by uncontrolled anger, easily frustrated, confrontational, and neither knew how to back down once they were mad. I knew about their arguments and verbal wars. Victor was one of those niggas that didn't appreciate a woman getting in his face and shit, while B was one of those chicks that stepped to a man as if she was one. He hailed from Compton, she was from the South side of Chicago. They were true products of where they came from. An Alpha male and female trying to be in relationship. I knew when they were beefing without either saying a word. When they were paired up to shoot a scene and were mad at each other; it was evident in the way they had sex. Angrily. Violently. Yet, they always made up and were crazy in love again.

****

At nine months in, I had ten full-featured videos under my belt. Six of them just featured me and other chicks from the roster, but four were my solo films. Tamani Black in *"Super Wet Pussy"*, *"Miss Juicy Booty"*,

"Head Game on 100 (Tamani's best blowjobs compilation)", and *"Triple Threat"*. That fourth video changed the game for me. It was two hours long, four scenes, and each scene was me and two niggas. We shot the video over the course of three days. Six different niggas licked, sucked, and fucked me from Friday night to Sunday evening. They dicked my mouth, between my tits, I jerked them off, got my ass ate out, and for the first time; I got DP'd. Double penetrated. A dick in my pussy and ass at the same time hurt like hell; but I had never orgasmed so hard before. My solo vids were stacking money in my bank account. I made $2000 per scene for the videos I was featured in, plus I was banking royalties from streams and downloads. My account was ridiculous! I always had no less than three-grand in cash on me, my wardrobe was out of this world, I was driving a brand-new car, and when not working out, shooting a scene, posing for photos, or with Brandi or Bryan; I was out doing me!

When everyone in my life was focused on themselves, I was able to go out and enjoy myself. By myself. I had to change my up appearance, but I still went out and had my fun. I possessed the money and freedom to do whatever I wanted to do; so that's what I did. I hit the mall to splurge, got my nails done on a regular basis, I went to the movies by myself, roller skating, to restaurants; even to the beach. I drove down to San Diego so I didn't run into any of my people and enjoyed two days of fun in the surf and sun. I hit a bar both nights. I got my drink on, smoked weed in a suite, snorted some coke, and hooked up. Twice. On the first night, I brought a Linebacker sized nigga with dreads and a huge dick back to my hotel. He was good in bed and I blew his mind with my mastery of fellatio. My second night in San Diego, after a day of chilling on the beach and an evening of bar hopping; I had a little tryst with a bad as chick from Costa Rica. Mami and I licked, sucked, and finger fucked all night long. Then I took my happy ass back to Los Angeles to resume my normal routine.

Life was all fun, sex, money and privilege for just over four years. I did close to a hundred featured scenes, forty-two solo videos, hundreds of LIVE web cam shows, a thousand photo shoots, and I traveled all over the place. We went on trips to NYC, Philly, Chicago, Miami, Atlanta, Hawaii, Puerto Rico, and Cancun. Some were for X-rated film events, but most of the time, it was for personal reasons or vacationing. Brandi and I traveled to have fun and shop, while Bryan took me with him to just have fun. We were at the Superbowl in New Orleans, the NBA All-Star game in Dallas, damn near ringside for a Pay-Per-View

Heavyweight title fight at the MGM Grand in Vegas, and we attended the BET awards in D.C. At this point in my life, I should have been perfectly content. Happy. Living my best life with no worries, troubles, or stress. On the outside, it looked like I was doing just fine. I was going on twenty-five, there were six digits in my bank account, I was a star in the adult industry, and I had everything I could ever want.

However, on the inside, I often felt hollow. From time to time, I felt used up. Exhausted. Unmotivated. Drained. Depression constantly nipped at my soul & spirit. Ninety-five percent of the time, I was under the influence of something. Alcohol, weed, cocaine, molly, and I was on & off with pills. Pain killers, sleep meds, and mood stabilizers. In public, I always put on a phony persona. My smiles were forced. I laughed when I didn't really want to. When I spoke during interviews and podcasts; no one knew what was going on inside. The turmoil and anguish of my past and the wall I built to keep that shit out was eroding. In private, when I was alone, I would get hit with such an intense wave of sadness; I would start crying without the ability to stop. Until I got drunk or high enough to force that dark and traumatic shit back down. Shooting scenes used to be so much fun for me. I craved the fire of hot, nasty sex. Those flames were slowly dying. More and more, sex with Bryan or my scene partners was just work. I rarely had an orgasm. I learned to fake them, I didn't get wet like I used to, and most of the time that I lied there getting fucked. I pretend moaned while feeling empty and lost.

In my off time, I was becoming a shut in. I would lie on the couch in sweats. Curled up, high as kite, watching TV. For hours on end. I would just lie there, blankly staring at whatever show or movie was on. I stopped masturbating, my appetite was up & down, my social life was sporadic, and I was frequently withdrawn from people. Even the two that I loved. Though I was still involved with Brandi and Bryan, my relationship with them was evaporating. B and Victor lived together, while Bry was quickly moving on from me. He was focused on his company and his other young girlfriend. A sweet looking brown skin chick named Myiesha from Texas. He found her when he went to Dallas for the Cowboys-Seahawks playoff game. They met at an afterparty. He brought her to LA to turn her into the next ebony porn star. Just like he did with me, he saw something unique in her and made Miss Iesha his. He and I fucked every so often, but I mostly saw him when shooting a scene. Which I was doing less and less as time went by.

As my popularity began to fade, Bryan or one of his people didn't hit my phone that often. I was sporadically contacted to schedule a photo shoot or plan a video. Pretty soon, I was only doing one or two scenes a month. It was getting harder and harder to fake it. Ergo, my videos were looked at differently. The comments online depressed me even more than I already was. Some wondered what was up with me. They said I looked robotic. Unexcited. Boring. Others were vile with their opinions. They spewed filth about my lack of intensity in my scenes. Saying that I lost my edge. I didn't bring the fire anymore. That I was burned out and wasting their damn time. My video trend numbers fell and fell with no sign of rising. HPP was invited to adult film events and no one called me to attend. The whole team went on vacation to Barbados. No one hit my phone to see if I wanted to go. Not even Brandi. When they got back, Bryan called me and asked me to come see him. At his office. He asked me straight up; Did I want out? Did I want to terminate my contract? I stared at him for a long ass time, feeling a strange sense of anger. Then it hit me square in the chest.

I meant nothing. Not to him, my so-called family with the company, or even to Brandi. I didn't even mean shit to myself. In that moment, as we sat across from one another; I finally realized the truth. I was nothing in this world. I was a broken, used up, emotionally shattered, irrelevant porn slut! The only time I meant something, the only time I was valued; was when I was catering to someone else. It started when I was teenager. A fifteen-year-old girl that fucked with a drug dealer. Then, I began fuckin' niggas for money. I turned that into a self-employed business. A call girl. Before my twenty-first birthday; I became a porno whore. I willingly let men and women use me, abuse me, degrade me, and drain the very life out of me. I attempted to drown every one of my demons with sex, drugs, alcohol, a lavish spending habit, and speeding through life in the fast lane. I was running. From my past. My demons. The pain that lived in my heart and spirit. Now, all of that shit has caught up with me and I was too tired to run anymore.

When I decided to opt out of my contract with High Power Productions, it was the end of my career in pornography. There had been several other production companies that attempted to steal me from Bryan over the years. Three were major in the game and I would have probably made much more money with them. Bad Angel Videos really wanted me to jump ship; but I was loyal. I was a nasty ass nymphomaniac; but I had loyalty in me. Something that didn't do me any good when I told Bryan that I wanted out. He just stared at me for a few seconds, nodded his head, then called Tia to begin the process. The process of terminating my contract with High Power. Before I left his office, I took one good final look at him. He never loved me. I don't think he even cared about me. He used to look at me with such sincere eyes and treat me like a kitten. Now, I saw indifference in his eyes as he shot me a monotone, *"Take care of yourself, Shanice."* I said nothing in return. I simply got up and walked out of his office.

I signed all of the contract termination papers, then a non-disclosure agreement. To not divulge any HPP internal information, slander the brand in anyway, or use the Tamani moniker or the on-screen likeness HPP Should I choose to sign on with another production company. Because I still had three individual un-produced on my contract; I lost all rights to the future revenue those videos would have generated. However, Tia made a call to the company's accountant. They still owed me royalties for past videos. Twenty-five percent my combined features & solo productions came out to $105,598. The accountant had that sum wired to my account and that was that. I was no longer an actress with High-Power Productions. No one said goodbye, hugged me, wished me well, or really looked at me as I left the production office. Instead of going home, I went for a drive around LA. I drove and smoked until it got dark. I ended up parked close to the beach near Santa Monica. I just sat there in my car with the music on, smoking one cigarette after another. Crying for over an hour. I was on my own, but I was not alone. I had company. It was just me and my demons now.

They were the friends that I didn't want, but were always there.

PART THREE

RESTORED HEART

"Sometimes,
You just have to die a little inside to be reborn.
Then rise again.
As a stronger and wiser version of you."

CHAPTER NINE

*"The hole is my heart is growing bigger by the day /
I wish that I could crawl inside, and hide away."*

-Cry, Alexx Calise

After spending weeks in a shell, not talking to a single person, and rarely leaving my apartment; I re-emerged. As something dark. The first thing I did was cover the ugliness brewing inside me. I hit the salon and got my hair done, then my nails. My next stop was to get a facial, my legs waxed, and then I shopped my ass off. Now that I was back on my bad girl shit; I partied. Hard. Almost every night, I hit up a bar or club. I got drunk & high, I flirted with men & women, I freak danced with both, and I unleashed the beast between my legs. I was straight wilding out. I hooked up with niggas and gave them head as they drove us to a hotel, then I blessed them with a night of nastiness that they'll never forget. Hot, rough, and violent sex that was more pain that satisfaction. I made niggas pull my hair extra hard, choke me, slap me, bend me, and drive their dick into me until I came. Over & over. I didn't want pleasure though. I wanted pain. Pain that hurt so good, it blocked out the shit trying to break my mind.

I was the same way with the women I hooked up with. I went home with lesbians and bi-sexual bitches for a night of sex they weren't ready for. I even scared a few of them with how aggressive and violent I was. When I was alone, I lived in the bottle. Or in a haze of marijuana smoke. Or, my body was numb from snorting lines of coke. I started to feel as if I was getting fat, so I went back to the gym and attacked my workouts like I was possessed. There were days that I sat in my place, in the quiet isolation with my cigarettes and liquor; staring at nothing as I fought a battle within my own mind. I tried and failed to keep the horrible memories out of my thoughts. Memories of my brother, my dad, being raped, losing Raheem, being separated from my best friend, and the imploded relationship I had with my mother. I had to pop pills to sleep, but when I slept, I had dreams and nightmares. I dreamt about the good times I had as a little girl with my family, going to the park with Avery, feeling safe with my father, and all of those laughter filled days when my mom did my hair.

My nightmares caused me to wake up in the middle of the night. Bathed in sweat, wide eyed, heart pounding in my chest. Screaming. I had night terrors about demons and beasts laughing as they grabbed me with their claws; but my reoccurring nightmare was of my uncle. The night he came into my room and forced his dick into me. In the nightmare, I tried to fight him off of me. Screaming for my dad as I kicked and pushed at him. Only for me to open my eyes, in my bed, realizing that I was actually crying and screaming for my mom in real life. This was how I developed insomnia. I would stay up for days. Only sleeping when I was physically unable to stay awake for another five minutes. I would then sometimes sleep for twelve, fourteen, sometimes eighteen hours straight. It didn't take long for the endless emotional tornado that I was trapped in to manifest physically. I always had a headache, my eyes frequently ached, my energy was up and down, and I would just burst into fits of crying.

I had been out of the loop for months, so I had no idea what was going on with the porn world. I didn't log on to the HPP website, I didn't surf the internet for smut anymore, I threw out all of my videos, deleted the files off my devices, and I didn't watch the news. I had deactivated my social media pages too. I also ditched my old phone. Thus, no one from the company could reach me on my new I-phone. They didn't have the number. One afternoon I was channel surfing when I stopped on a news report. Violence in the adult film business. Victor Dawkins, age 39, was arrested and charged with the murder of his girlfriend. Brandi Watts. Age 27. Both of whom were X-rated actors for High Power Productions. I sat there in state of quiet shock as the reporter informed me that my friend and former lover was dead and how she died. LAPD responded to a domestic violence call when neighbors heard Brandi screaming in her and Victors place. The cops arrived to find B beaten to bloody pulp and unresponsive. She was gone. Victor had fled their residence, but then turned himself in the next morning. He was charged with second-degree murder and Bryan Powers, the founder and CEO of High-Power Productions, declined to make a statement.

A week later, I went to visit Brandi. Her friends held a funeral for her and laid her to rest. I found out which cemetery she was buried in, brought her some flowers, and then sat with her. Crying my eyes out. I regretted not at least trying to take her with me when I left. She would have probably declined to leave the industry; but I should have at least tried. I did love her and she meant something to me. When I left, I considered asking her to walk away with me. Only I was too wrapped up in myself and deduced that she would have be unwilling to leave the lifestyle she was comfortable in. I hugged her headstone for a long time. Repeatedly telling her that I was sorry for what happened to her and that I broke our promise. I had sworn to take care of her. That nothing and no one would come between us. That I would never abandon her. I failed my friend and now I had to live with the fact that I didn't get to say goodbye. I didn't even call to check on her. I just left her and now she was dead. She followed my lead and I led her into a horrible death.

Two weeks after I visited Brandi, I got myself arrested. For beating a bitch ass in a club. I decided to go out to find a nigga to relieve the pressure and stress. One minute I was talking to a cute ass Crip nigga over a drink. Next thing I knew, some light skinned ratchet bitch was interrupting us. All loud and shit, getting in my face about *"her man"*. I didn't need the drama and publicity, so I picked up my drink and attempted to walk away from that messy situation. There were a hundred men in the club that night. I wasn't pressed about one. Miss Hood rat wanted smoke though. As I was walking away, the bitch brought the animal out of me. She barked at my back, *"That's right bitch! You better walk the fuck away!!"* She could have left it at that, but she decided to cross the line. By spitting on the side of my head. I sat my drink and purse on a table, turned, and went at that trifling bitch as if I was a Lion on a Gazelle. She wasn't ready for that and got her ass mauled for spitting on me. I whoop that chick ass until security pulled me off her as I was kicking and stomping a mud hole in her curled up, in the fetal position ass.

I fought with those security niggas too. I went the fuck off. Something sinister came out of me when that bitch violated me with her saliva. I was still tussling with the bouncers when the cops showed up. They restrained me, one of the security dudes gave them my purse, and I was led out of the club in handcuffs. I was kept in a holding cell until nine am the next morning. I was charged with a couple of misdemeanor offenses. Public disturbance, menacing, and disturbing the peace. I posted my own bond at my bail hearing, decided to plead guilty to all of the citations, and the judge hit me with a $1500 fine. I stopped by the clerk of court office, paid the fine with my Visa card, then left the courthouse with my paperwork. Only to see my face, well my old face, in the newspaper.

Former X-Rated Actress Arrested for Nightclub Brawl. The picture they used was from when I was known as Tamani Black, but they used my actual government name. It was out now. Anyone who knew me from my old life now knew what I've been doing. Even so, I didn't give a damn! They knew. So what?! So…the…fuck…what!!

Several hours after I left the courthouse, I was sitting in my apartment. I had showered and changed into something relaxing. I was sitting on the couch with some music on. Deep in my mind. Thinking about shit. I made a lot of money doing porn. Though I could simply leave LA, get myself right, and start over; I felt stuck. Trapped. Despite seeing an exit out of this Hell. I had the means to do something else with my life, but there was something in me that was preventing me from just getting up and doing it. Instead of packing up my shit and leaving this fucked up place; I just sat there on my couch. Dwelling on things. At some point, I started thinking about who I was? What I was? For the past decade, I was defined in the most grotesque manner. A pretty female that lived an ugly existence. My entire repertoire was predicated on sex, money, attention, and material possession. I liked to look good, but I felt bad inside. I loved to have a good time, with bad people. I was proud that I developed the sexual skills to make someone orgasm, but sex was just another addiction to me. A drug that I indulged in to feel something other than the misery, turmoil, and pain that resided in my heart and mind.

****

I came to the conclusion that I wasn't shit. A beautiful young woman that was broken inside and too afraid to face the pain and overcome it. I started thinking about all the various men I had sex with. For money, on camera, or as simply a one-night stand. I began feeling worthless as I remembered all the nasty shit I did and let them do to me. Cum on my face, in my mouth, all over my body; I let multiple men fuck me anally; spit on me; slap me around for the enjoyment of perverts that bought and downloaded my videos; I did public scenes where I took niggas into alley's or bathrooms and the cameraman recorded me sucking their dicks or engaging in a quick fuck for shock value. I ignored my tears as I recalled doing a gangbang with four motherfuckers. Pretending that I enjoyed it. Smiling brightly for the camera as the scene was wrapping up. I went to Bryan's sex parties and put on a masturbation show for everyone there. The sickest act of all was that I killed my own flesh and blood.

One of my partners impregnated me. I was so off my game that I slipped up with my birth control. We shot a scene where the guy I fucked busted two nuts in me. For me to show it oozing out to the camera. Porn creeps liked that kind of freaky shit. A little over two months later, I dropped a positive pregnancy test. I didn't say shit to anyone. I took some time off, made an appointment at a clinic, and had the fetus aborted. The fact that I terminated the life growing inside me didn't even hit me for two years. Yeah. The men that I've been with and encountered were savages; but so was I. I was a selfish, mentally fucked up, self-centered, morally bankrupt slut! After crying myself to sleep, I woke up around 8:30 pm. I downed a couple of shots, smoked a joint, got dressed, and went out. I didn't intend to pick anyone up, but I got so lit, that I allowed someone to pick me up instead. I was in a random bar on Sunset Blvd. Sitting by myself. Slow sipping a glass of henny while smoking a cigarette when a nigga took the stool next to me. That would be the moderately cute Russell.

He engaged me in small talk for a while, beating around the bush until he worked up the courage to let his desires be known. I wanted to tell him to get his lame ass the fuck out of my face. Instead, I chit chatted with him. Flashed a couple of smiles, flirted with him a little, drew him in, and then let it slip who I used to be. Tamani Black. His face lit up like a kid on Christmas as he claimed I did look familiar to him. He whispered that he used to jerk off to my videos and I was his favorite porn star. When I acted like what he said was a fuckin' compliment, that gave him the courage to take his shot. When he offered to pay me for an hour, my response made his night. I stubbed out my cigarette, finished my drink, and grabbed my purse before telling him, *"Let's go."* I followed him to a motel, he got us a room, we went in, and he got to live out his wettest wet dream. A regular dude got to fuck a chick that was a porn star. He once masturbated to my pussy. Now, he was in it. The lips that he used to watch other men cum all over; were now wrapped around his dick. Russell got his nut off, paid me, then he left. Once he was gone, something in me broke.

In the midst of trying to kill myself, I was half a second from slicing my wrist open; when suddenly, a face popped into my mind. Jamia. My best friend from childhood. It had been years since we spoke to or seen each other. In a fit of panic and need for a reason to live, I got on my phone and looked her up. I reactivated my Facebook page, found hers, and sent her a message. Because of the three-hour time difference, I had no choice but to wait for her to see my message. Hoping that she responded. I was asleep on my stomach when my phone woke me up. Someone was calling me through messenger. It was just after four am.

When I grabbed my phone and saw that it was Jamia; I quickly answered it. The very second that I heard my best friends voice, I started bawling. She did as well. For a while, we cried while trying to speak. Once we calmed down, I finally did it. I asked for help. I told Jamia that I needed help. That I was ready to kill myself. It truly felt that I had nothing to live for. I was tired and I needed someone in my corner to help me find my way out of the Hell I was stuck in. My bestie calmed me down and did what a best friend does.

By the time her plane landed at LAX, it was twelve hours later and I was sobered up. The moment she emerged from all the people exiting the plane; I rushed to her. Jamia and I hugged so damn tightly. I cried into her neck and she just held me. It felt like we stood there hugging forever. We finally left the gate, exited the terminal, walked to my car, and drove away from the airport. All the way to my apartment, I talked and she listened. The last time we saw one another, we were basically still kids. She went off to college and I went down a dark rabbit hole. Now, I was a former porn star and she was what she aspired to be. A college graduate with a business, married a good man, a mother of two, and she lived in a suburb's outside of Atlanta. We were nearly the same height now. She was also thicker than I last remembered her. She looked damn good. Healthy, alive, and in shape. We arrived at my place, she came in to help me pack some things, and then we left again. When stopped to eat, she made a call. To an inpatient mental health & suicide treatment center. Once she explained my situation to them, she was advised to bring me in. Immediately.

I agreed to be committed for a month. Thirty days to begin the path of getting myself right. Jamia was allowed to remain with me through the medical evaluation and intake process. I had to take a shower and change into a hospital gown, socks, and slippers. They gave me and my bestie ten minutes to speak before I was escorted to my unit. We hugged and cried again. Just before I was taken away, she cupped my cheeks with her hands, looked me in the eyes, and made me a promise. I wasn't going to go through this alone. I was not alone! I had her. She was going to be there for me. Jamia then kissed my cheek, told me be strong, and that she loved me. I walked away with the staff member and she escorted me to the first stop of my escape from Hell. The detox unit. For six days, I was a complete fucking mess. I had become dependent on drugs and alcohol without thinking I was addicted. That I had control of my vices. I didn't. They had control of me. Now that I was in a locked unit being monitored around the clock by a medical staff and mental health professionals, without being able to drink or get high; my system began to purge the physical craving.

I screamed, cried, threw up, shivered as if I was freezing, hurt all over, I pissed & shit on myself, and I screamed some more. I was unable to keep food or liquids down without vomiting. They had to insert an IV into my arm to keep me hydrated. Multiple times, due to my rage at not being able to drink, snort, smoke, pop a pill; I ripped the IV line out. I fought with the staff countless times. I screamed at them, cursed, spit, tried to hit them, threw up on them; but not once did they hurt me. Several had to hold me down to restrain me to the bed; but they were never mean or yelled at me. In fact, they tried to comfort me. They encouraged me to keep fighting. That the cravings will stop. When I was too weak to fight, one nurse even held me. She rocked me like a toddler while humming a soothing song. I thought a week had gone by, but it had only been three days. 72-hours. After three days of detoxing, the hard symptoms began to fade. Now, I was just sick. Exhausted. That was when they allowed Jamia to come in and sit with me. All day long. For three more days. I had two IV's, a heart monitor, an automated blood pressure cuff, lots of water, liquid food, and my best friend.

After six days in detox, I was cleared to be moved to one of the regular treatment units. I was given my clothing and hygiene stuff, then assigned to a room. With two other female patients. A white girl from Riverside and a black chick from Watts. I got along fine with my roommates and my days were spent in therapy. Group sessions and individual counseling. When not talking about what I had been through and listening to others share their stories; I was quiet. There was a TV room, but I barely went in it. I spent my time in my room or the reading area. They put me on anti-depressants and a mild sedative to help me sleep at night. I was pretty mellow most of the time. I was polite to the other patients, but I didn't get too close with anyone. I called Jamia in the evenings after dinner and she came to see me every Saturday afternoon. While the other patients were watching TV, playing board games, or cards during free time; I was either reading or sleeping. Unlike a lot of others, I always signed up to see a counselor for private therapy sessions.

Mine was a black woman that got deep with me. We spent every second of our hour-long session talking about me. My trauma, issues, thoughts, behavior, my brother, dad, mom, and my history with men. I cried a lot, often got mad, and when I ranted; she let me. Then, she circled me back a to the focus of the issue and we talked some more. I was diagnosed with bi-polar disorder, PTSD from the rape, acute anxiety, manic depression, and co-dependency. Maxine Daniels, my counselor, advised me in the strongest way possible to continue therapy after I was discharged. With all of the issues and layers of baggage that I was carrying; it was all but impossible for me to face all of that toxicity on my own and not destroy myself in the process. It was going to take a long time and a lot of work for me to reach a state of mind that even resembled normalcy. Yet, she confessed that she saw something strong in me. That I can overcome what I had been through. Everything that I did to myself and allowed myself to be subjected to. That I had it in me to come to terms with the trauma, come full circle with myself, and learn how to live again.

The weekend before I was discharged, Jamia came to see me that Sunday afternoon. I had wondered why I didn't see her on Saturday, but when she walked into the visiting room; I saw why. She didn't come alone. In her wake was my mother. My eyes welled up with tears as I dashed across the room and into her arms. Just like when I met Jamia at the airport, my mom and I hugged one another for a long time. Over and over, she just kept saying *"My baby." and, "I'm sorry."* Our visit went well. The three us talked about the old days, we smiled, laughed, and before they left at the conclusion of visiting hours; they told me that they'll be there bright and early to pick me up. The three of us hugged at the same time, cheeks were kissed, and I told my mom and besties that I'll see them in the morning. Before I went to bed that night, as I was packing up my stuff, Miss Daniels knocked on my door before she entered. She asked me for a moment of my time. I went with her and she escorted me off the unit. We went outside into the night behind the building. There was silver metal trash can by the door. She moved the can out some, then removed a folded sheet of paper from her pocket.

She handed it to me and I opened it. I looked down at myself. At what I used to be. Miss Daniels printed out a picture of me when I was Tamani Black. I was twenty-two-years old, on my knees on a bed, arms up with my hands behind my head, flashing a seductive, glossed lips smile with my violet contacts in. Wearing a tiny, black see-thru gown. I looked up at Miss Daniels as she handed me a lighter. As I accepted it, she spoke the truest words that anyone has ever said to me. She told me, *That girl in the photo is not you! That is a false and evil image of the beautiful young black woman standing before me. That girl is not you! She was never you! You will never be her! Now you burn that perverted image of a Queen! That was the work of the devil and you are no longer in Hell!*

That girl is not you, and will never be you! You are Shanice Landon!"
With silent tears rolling down my cheeks, I lit the corner of the picture
and dropped it into the can. I stood there and watched Tamani Black
burn to ashes.

Erasing her from my existence.

Forever.

EPILOGUE

It's been six years since I walked out of that psych hospital. Into the arms of my mother and best friend. My smile was ear to ear as I held them. Feeling reborn. I had no idea what I was going to do with the rest of my life, but I knew one thing for sure. I wasn't going to waste any more of it. The same day I was discharged from the center was the same day I made my departure from Los Angeles, California. Mom and Jamia had packed up my apartment and shipped my clothes and personal belongings to my new home until I was right with myself. We all went to lunch and then to the airport. I didn't look back at LA as we drove towards LAX. There was nothing I was going to miss about the City of Angels. I had fun times and memories of the city, but Los Angeles never knew the real me. People in LA knew Tamani Black. They never met Shanice. That's who I am. The girl they knew didn't exist anymore.

A few days after I was discharged, we boarded a plane and took off at 2:35 pm. 3,000 miles later. We landed at Hartsfield-Jackson international airport in Atlanta. Jamia's husband picked us up and I smiled at her after shaking his hand. She still liked tall and muscular dark-skinned men with dreads. Duane was a good-looking brother that had a genuine, gentleman vibe. He was very polite. We drove to their home where I met their kids and their baby sitter. Their grandmother on their fathers' side. Everyone welcomed me with open arms and warmth. Jamia's home was huge and there was a reasonably large guest house. My best friend had her husband set it up for me. I was staying with them as I continued to find myself and receive the help that I needed. My mom spent a few days in Georgia with us before flying back to Ohio. My new life began. For quite some time, I kept to myself. Jamia always checked on me out in the guest house, but she respected my need for privacy and let me be as I started the climb up that mountain within myself.

I didn't need to work at the moment, but I needed something to do. I signed up to get my GED and poured most of my time into reading. I came to love the quiet, tranquil atmosphere of the guest house. As I studied for my diploma, I went back to working out on a regular basis. I quit smoking too. I started running to begin healing my lungs. Twice a week, after I bought a new car, I drove to Atlanta for my therapy sessions. Jamia helped me find the perfect kind of professional for what I required. Dr. Joann Harris. My therapist. A wise and elegant black woman that specialized in treating black women with depression, PTSD, and survivors of sexual abuse. We met for an hour twice a week. She helped me face demons. Unpack the baggage of all the trauma I carried. She broke down all of my issues, we discussed them, I cried a well of tears, and we made progress. By the time I earned my GED and was talking about college with Jamia; I was becoming the woman I needed to be. At the stern advice of my mom, best friend, and therapist; I refrained from dating. Or even flirting with men.

I got hit on all the time, but I didn't allow a man into my space. Whether I was out for a run, shopping, at the library, or hanging out with my best friend and her kids; dudes took their shot with me. Yet, I never responded to their flirting. Though I did not disrespect them while rejecting their advances; I never gave them my number. Though I still had a Facebook page, I was rarely on it. I seldom, if ever posted anything. When I did, it wasn't a sexy selfie anymore. I shared quotes or motivational pictures. I used to crave attention; but those days were gone. I stayed on the path that I needed to be on. The path of healing, becoming a better person, learning to love myself, and building a core of serenity within my soul. I focused on my future. Now that I had one. Not long after earning my GED, I enrolled in community college to pursue an ambition that my mother and Jamia convinced me was absolutely perfect for me. My time was spent studying, doing research, homework, writing term papers on my laptop, preparing for exams, and I lived in the campus library.

I gave my ambition everything I had for four long years. Earning my Associates and then my Bachelor's degree. In Mental & Behavioral Health Sciences. Less than a month after graduation, I began my new job. As an advocate & counselor at a women's outreach center in Atlanta. I made the decision to dedicate my life to something bigger than myself; once I found peace. I came to terms with my past, forgave myself, let go of the pain, and found a cause to fight for. Helping other black girls like me. Young sisters that were broken inside. From being abused, violated, and steered towards a path that leads to self-destruction. I became the person they can turn to. Trust. Help them learn to stand up again. Fight. Rise from their ashes of their misery. Find something in this life to smile about. That was my life now and has been for the past two years. I was now thirty-two-years old and my life was about helping others. For eight to twelve hours a day, I counseled young black girls in my office. None of them knew what I used to be, but I did share one thing about myself that we had in common.

I also fell into a dark rabbit hole. While running from the pain. Trying to hide from my demons. Now, it was my responsibility to teach them how to climb out of that hole. One inch at a time. I survived Hell. It was now my job to show other young black women that they could too. There is a way out of Hell. A path out of self-destruction. I was a living testament of that truth. Saving young black girls is what I've dedicated my life to. This was my mission now. My cause. My sole purpose for the rest of my days. Taking in broken baby birds and returning them to the freedom of the sky. I help them heal their broken wings until they learn how to fly again. This is the reason I survived. The reason I didn't find death.

Helping young black Queens find their crown is my true calling in life.

THE END

Thank you for your support, it is truly appreciated, and if you haven't read any of my other books, here is the full list of my titles:
(All available on Amazon)

-Hood Royalty Series
(Queen of Diamondz, Queen of Diamondz II,
King of Spadez, Royal Reign: The Finale)

-Power & Justice
-Power & Justice: Backlash
-Power & Justice: Backlash II
-Power & Justice IV: N.J.N.P
-Power & Justice: Final Solution
-Brother's & King's
-Natural Born Ryderz
-Natural Born Ryderz II: Death Before Dishonor
-Legacy of the Master
-Let It Burn
-Venomous Fruit
-Legacy of a Champion: PART ONE
-Legacy of a Champion: PART TWO
-Loving This Woman Right
-Loving my Man Right: Kazim & Mekena Part II
-Soul of a Menace: a Thug Life Story
-COLD as ICE
-Queen's of Death: The Final Option
-Mr. Inferno
-Mr. Incredible
-Safire: The fall of an angel
-Jaguar: Memoirs of a Bad Girl
-When a King Loves a Queen
-You Belong to Me
-Seductive Flavors: An interracial erotica love story
-Naughty Girls
-Touching Fire
-Pain & Pleasure: A story of Money, Sex, & Misery

<u>Novels can be purchased on</u>:

www.amazon.com

<u>Author can be contacted at</u>:

E-mail: tylegend365@gmail.com
Instagram: tyrob3428
Facebook: Ty Robinson / e-mail: tylegend365@gmail.com
Twitter: @authorTyRob

BLACK REIGN
PUBLISHING

www.ingramcontent.com/pod-product-compliance
Lightning Source LLC
Chambersburg PA
CBHW081256130726
47998CB00010B/2826